Meet Me
in
Moonshine

WTP

First published by Wattle Tree Press, Australia, 2023.
www.wattletreepress.com

This paperback edition published 2026.

A catalogue record for this book is available from the National Library of Australia

NATIONAL LIBRARY OF AUSTRALIA

Meet Me in Moonshine: a novella
Cover: Melody Jeffries Design
Editor: Sue Copsey
ISBN: 978-0-6456910-0-9 (paperback)
ISBN: 978-0-6456910-1-6 (ebook)

This novella is dedicated to my parents.
I love you both to the moon and back.

... And also to anyone I ever said I'd dedicate a book to.
I kept my promises. You're all my favourite.
You're welcome.

Meet Me in Moonshine

A MOONSHINE ROMANCE NOVELLA

BROOKLYN DEAN

WTP

Author's Note

This book is best paired with a strong coffee and a sweet bakery treat, or a beer and pie. Treat yourself!

For additional adult reading fun, enjoy reading Jillian's story whilst naked in a pool. If anyone asks why you're reading in the nude, just say you were 'getting into character' and blame Jillian, not me! (Alternatively, a bath will work, too. Actually, it's legally preferred.)

If bookish treats and skinny dipping aren't your thing, may I suggest a different type of holistic reading experience? I have created a Spotify playlist for you to enjoy as you read. Scan the QR code to start listening.

Lastly, thank you for being here. You are intelligent, wise and clearly very good looking. I hope you enjoy meeting Jillian and her Mystery Man. Meet you back in Moonshine soon!

♡ Brooklyn Dean

Content Warnings

Dear Reader,

While this book is intended to be a romance (usually soft and fluffy by the mere nature of the genre) it does contain some potentially sensitive topics you might like to be aware of.

Please be advised that *Meet Me in Moonshine* contains:

- death of a family member (mentioned),

- unwanted physical contact (one instance),

- crude language (AKA Australian English), and

- some horribly misspelled text messages.

Monday

A MERI DISCOVERY

IT HAD JUST TURNED 6pm when Friday's Café got its second wind. Bursting to life, the speakers blared Aussie rock legends, The Angels. 'Am I Ever Gonna See Your Face Again' lit up the café like it was midnight at the pub. Everyone stood, throwing their arms into the air, gyrating, and headbanging in time with the beat.

Friday's caffeinated customers danced wildly, the sudden movements nearly knocking the frail Mrs Johnson sideways in her walker as she bopped with the best of them.

Jillian Maitland leaned against the old-fashioned cash register, smiling at the only other stationary person in the popular café – the proprietor himself, Friday.

Whoever chose The Angels was a dead-set legend.

Seeing Mrs Johnson letting her white hair whip back and forth as she headbanged next to her cherubic grandson, who clapped on in awe, had just made Jillian's entire year.

As the track finished and the volume returned to normal, the crew began transforming the café into its evening incarnation as an arts space for hire.

Giggling customers righted their ruffled clothing, smoothed down hair, and gathered their things to leave. Friday breathed deeply, passing Jillian her extra-tall double shot cappuccino. Sure, it was late in the day for the massive caffeine hit, but sleep was for the weak.

"Friday, you're my hero."

He never forgot her sickly sweet order – double caffeine injection, a shot of vanilla, cinnamon, and extra chocolate dusting on top. "Wonderful, as always," she sighed blissfully, sliding her frequent sipper's card across the wooden bench.

"Freebie again," Friday commented, punching a new hole through the cardboard then handing it back to her. "You know, Jillian, it's great that you come in every day, but I get the feeling you're either here or at work and nowhere in between. It'd be nice to see you out and about a bit more."

Concern laced his tone. Jillian tried, and failed, to find a response. Her eyes briefly darted up to his, and he cleared his throat pointedly, changing the subject.

"Want a book with your brew? I got a new MERI bundle delivered this morning." Friday pointed towards the brimming bookcase tucked into the corner at the end of the counter. "There's a few interesting reads in there. All different genres this time, not just fifty shades of Mills and Boon."

Jillian laughed, remembering Friday's embarrassment at the selection and his shock at its popularity with his customers – particularly the very lively Mrs Johnson, who had insisted on reading passages to him over her daily pot of tea. Hearing her old teacher's frail voice reading smut aloud in the café had been one of the few things to bring a smile to Jillian's face lately. Those MERI moments, and Friday's caffeine injection, were bright glimmers of light in her otherwise dull days.

The Moonshine Easy Reading Initiative, MERI for short, ensured five lucky local businesses would enjoy a rotation of literature from the Moonshine Municipal Library. The 'easy reading' part was the fact that people didn't actually have to *go to* the library to find their books. Literature had been made widely accessible throughout the small town. 'In sight, in mind. MERI reading, Moonshine', boasted their official motto.

Being free, easily accessible, and in the town's most frequented stores, made the reading scheme a tremendous success. More Moonshine locals were reading than ever before, according to the frequently run ads on The Cat and the Fiddle FM.

The quirky local radio station was named for the DJ's two favourite things – the cat who often interrupted live-to-air streaming with raucous, demanding purrs, and the classical fiddler's music that prompted listeners to call in for competition time.

"So, do you want to take home a new read?" Friday nodded encouragingly toward the bookshelf.

Jeez, let me think. Will Oscar Wild let me snuggle in bed with a book?

Oscar was her cat. Well, not *her* cat. He was wild, hence his last name. Oscar was a grey, silky-furred night prowler who often claimed her bed as his own. Like a secret lover, Oscar would creep up the latticework beyond her bedroom window and slide into her room, sharing his warmth and her blankets. Which, in the middle of an Australian summer, was both comforting and disgusting.

She wasn't sure if cats sweat like humans, but she did know the ball of radiating heat he produced made it difficult for her to sleep. At least she had company.

An almost-thirty-year-old woman, wondering if my non-pet cat will care if I bring a book home? Dear Jesus, I need a life.

It wasn't the first time she'd thought about widening her world again, but no. Not now. She still wasn't ready. Her heart still hurt too much. Letting anything else or any*one* else in would just exacerbate the ache she carried in her chest.

"A new random read sounds lovely." Jillian thanked Friday, sipping deeply with an almost giddy moan as the delicious double-strength caffeine settled into her very soul. Anything was possible, even healing a broken heart, if you had a decent coffee in your system.

Jillian slid past the delicious goodies in the cabinet, eyes already on her prize. Thumbing the book spines, Friday's liquid magic settled warm and soothing, deep within her.

Absorbed in the titles, she barely noticed the café's transformation. Tonight was *Paint with a Pint*, or so said the A-frame sign Friday had placed outside. Moonshine had a long history of liquor-love, but the painting aspect of the event was seen as a bit 'posh' by some of the locals, who equated beer more with soggy-carpeted bar scenes than art.

The tangy smell of hops began to float through the air and the excited murmuring of the painters setting up their easels jolted Jillian back to reality. A careful deliberation of which book to take home to Oscar wasn't a possibility this evening.

Grabbing a random title from the shelf, Jillian turned, and walked face-first into the paint-aproned front of a solid mass of man. Her hand clenched around the already squished cup in her hands as his beer caressed her chest in a chilled rush. Hot and cold liquids trickled down to her knickers, soaking her summer dress.

"Jesus! Oh!"

Jillian's dignity dropped into the warm mixture of coffee and beer that was forming a frothing, wee-coloured puddle on the floor.

"Jeez, miss, I'm so *so* sorry." The man stepped back.

Looking down, Jillian's jaw dropped. The red and white love-hearts of her underwear were showing through her dress, where it stuck in semi-transparent patches to her body. Grip failing, her cup hit the floor. The coffee splashed her knees, meeting the man's beer as it dribbled down her legs.

It feels like I've pissed myself.

"I am so sorry, really. Let me help." The man doubled over to collect their slain cups, at the same time Jillian bent to wipe her legs. *Thunk.* Their foreheads collided spectacularly.

More heads turned as the disaster intensified.

"Shit, you guys okay?" Friday's familiar Converse All-Star sneakers entered her limited vision as he rushed across with a mop. Head throbbing, face red and her will to live ebbing, Jillian plucked the stained dress away from her dripping body. Tears pricked her eyes.

I smell like a brewery.

"Miss, I ..." The Coffee-Killer began wiping his hands down her legs, flicking liquid to the floor.

Thank God I shaved this morning.

His braided bracelet caught her eye, the two small blue beads clicking together as his hands worked up and down her calves. She had seen many of these in town lately. Even Friday wore one.

The bracelets were part of a local fundraiser for men's mental health, an initiative run by Fit But, a popular local gym. It was a worthy cause, in Jillian's opinion. Too many lives were lost in rural towns like Moonshine, because of some outdated hypermasculine desire for 'strong' (silent) farmers. So, this Coffee-Killer was a nice guy, in some respects at least. And now he was sliding his hands up and down her sticky beer-and-double-shot-cappuccino legs.

Oh my God, this is so embarrassing.

"Please, I ..." *want you to stop –?*

Despite the circumstances, this was the first time a man had touched her legs in well over a decade. Ten. Whole. Years. *Oh, Jesus, has it really been that long?* That realisation alone flooded her with horror.

His warm hands curved around her shins, sliding up and down diligently, flicking droplets to the floor.

"Stop," she said weakly, gripping her MERI book tighter. "I … I have to go."

He wore neat brown dress shoes, she noted as she stepped back, the sticky warm mix squelching in her sandals. No way had the caffeinated beer concoction soaked through his professional Oxfords. Her, on the other hand …

Too embarrassed to meet the Coffee-Killer's or Friday's eyes, Jillian raced out of the café and into the evening.

Unwilling to skulk through town in a soaked dress, she headed for the Moonshine Municipal Library, found a quiet corner (but weren't they all?) and sobbed, with only two million pages witnessing her meltdown.

By the time she trudged up to her front gate, dusk had slipped into an inky, star-filled night.

Oscar waited, impatiently mewling to be let in, and her dress was now dry. Ruined, but dry. Still squelching, Jillian kicked her sandals off by the door as it swung open. Pushing his way past, without so much as a thankful meow, the cat practically skipped up the stairs to Jillian's bedroom.

Sighing, she shook her head at the cat. "You're the only man dying to get into my bed, Oscar."

Sliding off her dress and underwear, Jillian kicked them into the laundry. Still gripping the MERI book, she considered following Oscar up to bed, but decided instead to pad to the pool.

Skinny-dipping at night was one of her favourite summer activities. She had read somewhere that Australians were to water like fish were to the sea. In her case at least, the analogy applied. Sliding into the pool, she sent a silent prayer of thanks to the Gods of High Fences and old-fashioned, distanced residential blocks for enabling her naked, wet frivolity.

Summer in Moonshine was always blistering, and the air conditioner was a luxury she couldn't afford.

Slipping up to her waist in the blissfully cool water, Jillian settled into her favourite spot. Cold tiles kissed the underside of her elbows as she leaned back, the book held carefully away from the water. Taking three deep breaths, she looked to the waxing moon.

In almost two weeks, it would be Valentine's Day.

Eleven days until *The Day*. Eleven days until her single sadness would manifest in a bucket of double choc chip ice-cream and sobbing into Oscar's uncaring silvery body. And only eleven days until her unfortunately timed birthday.

It was a sick cosmic joke, sharing her birthday with Valentine's Day, when cupid's arrow constantly evaded her.

As the only child of a loveless marriage, the romantic tone of her birthday felt like tiny stitches across her heart. Stitches that strained, tugging too tight to close the gap left with every boyfriendless year that passed by.

"I'm not looking forward to this one," she told the man in the moon. "Thirty. Thirty! I thought I'd have a husband, maybe a baby, a stable career by now. Instead ..."

Her eyes slid to the open window of her bedroom, where Oscar would be lounging.

Her fingers were ringless.

And as much as she loved her job at Bloomin' Brilliant (the town's best florist) and her occasional shifts at The Pope (Moonshine's first and longest continually licensed tavern), arranging flowers and pouring beers weren't exactly her dream roles.

"Ha!" Jillian laughed to herself. "Dream job. What is that?" She had never found any *one* thing she wanted to spend her life doing. Unlike most of her classmates, who were settled and stable as cruise ships by now, Jillian felt more like the *Titanic*. Breakable, drifting, sinking into an icy sea.

She sunk further into the cool pool.

"Where's the excitement in my life? The thrill? The love of the season?"

The neighbour's dog barked in response. A cat – she hoped not Oscar – shrieked back.

"Not bloody here," she mumbled to the glowing, blue-lit pool. It lapped at her chest as she rolled slightly to examine her MERI book: *Meet Me in Moonshine*.

Oh great, another local colonial history book.

As one of Australia's first townships, following the arrival of the first fleet in the 1800s, Moonshine often found itself the subject of historians whose interest spanned the familial generations, period architecture or illegal liquor culture it was named for.

Long ago, she had found an outdoor lamp to read by. Flicking it on, Jillian flipped through the front matter, searching for the tell-tale historical society logo. A slip of bright red paper caught her eye. A bookmark, maybe? Extracting the red page, a slow smile spread.

Dear Reader ...

A hand-written note! She loved little treasures like this. The subtle, personal touches a thoughtful someone had left behind. Tiny pieces of humanity filled her heart with hope.

Like when Friday left a 'have a great day' message on her coffee cup, or the young lad at the farmers' market who always threw in her brussel sprouts for free, claiming no one else ate them anyway.

Once, someone had left a tab with the grocer and she'd received half her weekly shop for free, thanks to that random act of kindness.

Jillian adored loving inscriptions in second-hand books, and that 'free hugs' guy who simply wanted to make someone's day a bit brighter.

The baker, 'Big-Bellied' Ben, was her all-time favourite. His standard fare was the baker's dozen, charged at the price of a twelve-pack. Jillian could put away thirteen sweet buns over the course of a fortnight ... okay, more like a week. She'd eat one ... *okay, maybe two* ... on the first day, then freeze the rest.

Thinking of the treat in her freezer, her stomach growled. The sticky beer and coffee had washed off her skin, and fruit bats had started to glide silently overhead.

It suddenly struck her as immensely pitiful that, were she to drown right here and now, nobody would likely notice. Her boss at Bloomin' Brilliant might pop around after a few days, but as a casual worker, her absence wouldn't be noted for a while.

Loneliness replaced the pleasure of the pool's calming freshness. Tiny waves were trying to swallow her up. Swimming alone, naked, in cold water on a hot summer's evening, had suddenly lost its allure.

No, Jillian. Stop the pity party.

Sliding out, into the warm, dry evening, she quickly towelled off before heading inside to find herself some sugary sustenance, and maybe finish reading the little red note. Climbing onto the bed, licking icing sugar from her lips, Jillian snuggled down with her MERI book moments later.

Dear Reader,
Are you in need of a little adventure? A mystery? Something a little different? If you are, turn to page 50. Go on, I dare you.

Giggling, her mouth full of sticky bun and Oscar purring around her ankles, Jillian flipped through the pages of the book.

Yep, another history of my hometown.

It seemed to be a faces-behind-the-places kind of history, personal stories linked to iconic architectural features, with hand-drawn illustrations, old photographs, and newer ones of restoration projects. It was a beautiful book. Not something she would normally pick up, but still. She found page fifty. Another red note awaited.

Oh, hello. Nice to see you again. I see you, like me, need a little more than the everyday Moonshine life experiences.

Before we go any further, I should explain myself clearly. I am a 28-year-old man who enjoys the company of women, and I don't want to feel lonely anymore. If you are a woman who likes men, and who might like a 28-year-old one more specifically, skip to the next paragraph.

If this does not describe you, please do me a favour and return this note to the book, then send **Meet Me in Moonshine** *back to the shelf you found it on. Hey, I get it, this book is interesting! I would've picked it up off the shelf too! But please – help a brother out.*

This was not exactly what she'd expected. A little further down the red page, the note continued:

Still here? Intrigued? Let's play a little game. A scavenger hunt if you will. In the pages of this book, leave me a note about yourself and your favourite place in town. Then leave Meet Me in Moonshine *at my favourite place in this town. (Hint, it's pictured here.)*

Here? Did he mean in the book? Jillian examined page fifty, on which there was a black and white photograph of The Moonshine Whine. Is that where the book was supposed to travel to now?

Over the next half hour, Jillian pondered the note, its intention, and clues as to its writer. One thing was certain, each time she read the words *I don't want to feel lonely anymore*, her heart leapt into her throat.

Me neither, Mystery Man. Stroking the book cover gently, she said out loud, "Me neither."

Oscar, jealous of the attention the book was receiving, pushed his nose between her hand and the cover, sliding himself under her palm.

"Oscar." She stroked his soft fur affectionately. "It's kind of comforting, in a sad way, to know there's someone out there who's as lonely as us." The grey-furred boy pushed himself up her leg, indifferent eyes blinking.

"I think it's time I tried a *human* boyfriend," she sighed apologetically, the red note suddenly heavy between her fingertips. "Maybe even a blind date ... with a book."

Tuesday

THE MOONSHINE WHINE

THE MOONSHINE WHINE STOOD tall and observant on the town's tallest pimple of a hill. It was a joke – a lighthouse shining its brilliant beam over the inland town. There was no airport, or reason for such a landmark, yet there it was, its light slicing through the air, reaching out in longing for the ocean that waved, teasing, over two hour's drive East.

'The Whine' was so-called because the town's early European settlers had complained ceaselessly about the surprising steepness of the small hill, or so local legend explained. It was a make-out spot for local teenagers at night and saw a small number of tourists by day. The only other people journeying up The Whine were lycra-clad runners and cyclists – the kind of over-enthusiastic men and women who put up with screaming calf muscles and rolled ankles from the uneven terrain. Jillian was certainly not in any of those categories.

The last time she'd visited The Whine was on a school excursion when she was six. She had argued with the teacher about the purpose of the lighthouse.

"It's Rapunzel's tower, you Muppet," Jillian had said, arms crossed and poking out her tongue. It had been her first (and last) detention. Apparently comparing the teacher to Gonzo, in front of the whole class and a small tour group of elderly people, was frowned upon.

Now, as she swung her Suzuki Swift into one of the many empty, weed-spotted car parks, she saw The Whine with fresh eyes.

Her Mystery Man liked this place. Actually, he'd written it was his *favourite* place in Moonshine. How strange. Maybe there was something here she hadn't noticed before.

Cutting the engine, she breathed the last few seconds of icy air, opening the door reluctantly. The full force of the Australian summer heat hit her instantly. Somewhere in the distance, a kookaburra laughed as she slid on her sunglasses and hat, attempting to avoid the sun's bite.

Why am I doing this? Doubt over this plan's sanity settled under her skin. Pros and cons tossed in her brain. *It can't hurt,* she rationalised. *It's just a bit of fun. And Jesus, I need some fun to shake up these doldrums.*

A small group of people gathered at the entrance to the tall, sandstone tower.

"You here for the tour?" asked an old man she recognised as a customer of Bloomin' Brilliant.

"Tom, right?"

"Yeah ..." He looked at her suspiciously.

"Jillian Maitland, from the flower shop. I delivered your order for fifty red roses for your fiftieth wedding anniversary a few weeks ago. I hope Delilah loved your thoughtful gift."

His face melted at the mention of his wife. "Oh, yes, she surely did. The house smelled of roses for weeks, it was so lovely." He gently patted her hand. "So, are you here for the tour?"

"If I can ..."

"Oh no bother, no bother. Just tack onto this group here. My treat, for the wonderful way you arranged that bouquet. Beautiful, it was, just beautiful, though not as lovely as my Delilah. Fifty years of marriage!" He shook his head, grinning ear to ear.

This is the kind of enduring love story I want.

Jillian watched the old lover's smile, lingering as a younger man began the tour.

"See you soon, Jillian!" Tom called, one hand raised in parting. "Valentine's Day is just around the corner, after all, and I'll need at least one more rose for my Delilah."

Jillian had mentally prepared herself for a dull history of the (blessedly cool) sandstone lighthouse, yet it turned out to be surprisingly informative and engaging.

The young man leading the tour, maybe sixteen she guessed, from his pimpled face and sometimes squeaky tone, obviously knew his local history. Importantly, he knew how to entertain a crowd with witty anecdotes about The Whine's colourful past, filling the tour with laughter and awe at tales of bootleggers and bushrangers who used the site as somewhat of a Northern Star, aiding their illegal endeavours.

The tour finished at the top of the old tower, where the group was invited to explore the displays in the circular lantern room, before making their own way back down the stairs. In the lantern room, massive reflector panels, lamps and lenses were already spinning, ready to create Moonshine's evening beacon.

The small tour group dispersed, examining miniature township models in glass cases, historic documents kept safe behind ancient frames, and a small collection of rocks, stones, and even some fossils found in the vicinity.

Jillian's eyes, however, landed squarely on a small piece of red paper, folded neatly and slipped between the jagged cracks of the sandstone bricks. Wiggling the paper loose, she smiled as she read.

Hello Dear Reader,

The Moonshine Whine is magnificent, isn't she?

Jillian cast her eyes through the enormous windows of the dome overlooking the sprawling town beyond. Moonshine's highest vantage point offered an unparalleled view.

"She really is." Jillian smiled, returning her gaze to the red slip of paper.

Though I'm sure she isn't as lovely as you.

Heat rose in her cheeks, and it had nothing to do with the sun biting through the glass at the top of the lighthouse. Her Mystery Man was a charmer.

Wait – *her* Mystery Man? When had she started thinking of the twenty-eight-year-old Whine lover as *hers*?

Now it's your turn. I left a spare slip of paper with Tom, the lighthouse keeper. Leave me a note, Dear Reader, if you're interested in continuing this journey. Slip it into the book and leave it with Tom.
With anticipation … Meet me in Moonshine.
D-

So, her Mystery Man's name started with D? Derek? Donald? How many 28-year-old lonely men did she know whose names started with D? Or was it a pseudonym?

Her heart *thunk*ed heavily. *I'm lonely, too, Mr D.*

Fumbling for a pen in her handbag, she started her reply.

Dear D,
This is an unusual way to make a new friend, but honestly,
I think I needed this in my life. Both the adventure and the
friend, that is.

She paused, wondering just how much to commit to paper.

I often feel lonely too. Thank you for the lovely tour of The
Whine. I've lived in Moonshine all my life and never really
appreciated this place until today.

My favourite place in Moonshine is the Queen's Rose
Garden. Few people know the age of the twisted bushes.
They're among the oldest living things in town. Many of
those roses survived their First Fleet voyages from England.
They outlived countless convicts and free settlers on those
journeys to the colonies. Like The Whine, they'll survive the
test of time.

She paused again, then carried on, shrinking her handwriting to fit onto the small square of paper.

BROOKLYN DEAN

I don't really know how this works, but I'll leave **Meet Me in Moonshine** *with the Lighthouse Keeper Tom. If he tells me the book was collected, I'll go the Queen's Rose Garden tomorrow to find you.*

That sounds wrong. Jillian added an 'r' to her last word, then concluded her letter: **your reply.**
Sincerely,
J–
PS. I'm an almost 30-year-old woman. I hope my age isn't a turn-off...
I am straight, like long walks on the beach and random scavenger hunts through Moonshine. Lucky you.

Wait, was she *flirting*? Before she could over-analyse this whole ridiculous activity, Jillian slid her note into *Meet Me in Moonshine* and hurried to locate Tom.

Wednesday

FOR ALL THE ROSES

It was Wednesday. 'Hump Day,' she'd heard it called. The hilly peak of the week, when everything seemed to ramp up and become increasingly difficult before the welcome downward slope to the weekend. And the only *hump* happening was the slowly ticking hands of the clock Jillian had been trying *not* to stare at since 9am. All she needed was for today to fast-forward to 3pm. Home time. Hump completed. Time to go to the Queen's Rose Garden off Argyle Street, locate *Meet Me in Moonshine* and read the next red note from D.

After leaving the book with Tom the day before, she had returned to find it gone, collected by her Mystery Man. Sure, she could have telephoned, if The Whine had been connected to modernity. But it wasn't. So, for the second time in twenty-four hours, Jillian made the trek up The Whine. Old Tom himself cackled when she'd asked for his mobile number.

"No point," he'd wheezed cheerily, "no reception up here anyway, so it's a good thing you came up."

"Can't tell you much about him," Tom had slyly added, "... 'cept he's tall. Dark hair, like yours. That's it! Not saying more!" He had thrown his hands up and walked away into the depths of the lighthouse.

Leaving the identity of the Mystery Man to her imagination was a recipe for a restless night. Jillian had dreamed of all the tall, dark-haired celebrities she had ever seen in a film, TV show or gracing the cover of the world's sexiest magazine for horny single women – *Men's Health*.

It had been a long night with such ruminations, but today seemed to have slowed time even further.

Her morning coffee at Friday's Café took forever as Jillian questioned her favourite barista about the books.

"All I know is they came from the library with the MERI programme," he said. "I don't remember that particular book." His dark eyes flicked to the bookshelf in the corner. "But the only thing I ever really read is a menu or recipe book, so I'm not much help."

Jillian had trudged to work, hot coffee sitting heavily in her stomach and a nervous sweat threading across her brow.

At 2pm, the thermometer hit 39 degrees. The misting pedestal fans in Bloomin' Brilliant were the only thing keeping the remaining floral arrangements and staff alive. Patches of sweat made her sunflower dress cling in awkward, uncomfortable places. Jillian dreamed of her pool, wondering absently where her feline boyfriend spent his days.

"Got somewhere to be?" her boss, the rather ironically named Iris Bloom, asked as Jillian glanced yet again at the clock. Wilting like the flowers, Iris was waving a flyer back and forth in front of her face, to little apparent effect. Iris had a hippy vibe about her. She floated around in life, all fragrant layers and freckles from long summers spent in the sun.

"Oh, um ... Jesus. I'm so sorry, Iris, I–"

"Don't you worry, honey." The corners of Iris' blush-pink lips turned up. "I'm glad you finally have something you're watching the clock for, love. You deserve a bit of excitement in your life." Iris handed Jillian her handbag with a quick wave of her flyer-fan. "Now, you take those pretty brown eyes off the clock and onto the road. Go home, Jillian," she said. "Or wherever else it is you want to be going."

Giving Iris a quick peck on the cheek, Jillian took the offered bag, removed her car keys, and sped towards her favourite place in town.

The Queen's Rose Garden was one half of the town's biggest parkland, set three blocks back from the main street and straddling the winding Wollundry River.

In a word, it was majestic. The gardens had been designed with strolling, eligible lords and ladies in mind, with wide paths circling inward towards a tall, multi-tiered fountain that always reminded Jillian of an elaborate wedding cake. The stone edges of every path were lined with multi-coloured petunias and fluffy, soft, lamb's ear plants. Beyond those were the roses that had, when she was a girl, stretched to Jillian's height and taller.

She'd always marvelled at the ancient, twisting trunks of the bushes, the thorny stalks topped with impressive, colourful, and highly scented flowers.

"Roses aren't as fragrant, nowadays," she lamented to a huge 'Penny Lane', inhaling deeply. "You're magnificent," she told the soft yellow petals, eyes scanning the gardens.

The sun beat down from the cloudless blue sky. Not a whisper of breath stirred the leaves. A sweet haze of delicate perfume filled the air. For a few long moments, Jillian soaked up the serenity. The chirp of tiny happy birds, the buzzing bees, and the fragrant atmosphere stilled her soul.

Suddenly, she was very aware of being alone.

No time for self-pity, she told herself, scanning the gardens in earnest for the familiar green and gold book. Normally, the rose gardens calmed her, but with the hunt on for *Meet Me in Moonshine*, excitement and anticipation filled her veins.

What would he write? Where would he send her to explore? What tiny detail about himself might he leave her?

Lost in thought, she didn't hear the shuffling on the path behind her until it was too late. A knobbly hand reached out, snaking around her shoulder.

With an almighty scream, her world tilted away from the clutching fingers and Jillian fell into the petunias, her arse half in the garden and half on the path.

"Ow!" Looking up, she saw the weathered hand reaching down to help her up.

"Oh, *cara mia*, I didn't mean to scare you!" Moonshine Council's dedicated gardener, Giovani Luca, pulled her up with a surprisingly strong heave. "Give me a hug! Haven't seen you for a long while, *bella*!" The scrawny man wrapped his long arms around her, holding her tightly for a brief moment. Giovani was a stooped man whose limbs were as gnarled as the old rose bushes he tended.

"Sorry, Mister Luca. I've been ... busy." She hated lying to the old Italian fellow, but how could she possibly say that flowers were better friends than people? That she'd been trying to make a conscious effort to engage with humanity again? That, despite how lovely his meticulously maintained roses were, since the passing of her mother they made her sad?

"Not a worry, I understand. A young *dolcezza* like you must have a string of boyfriends and girlfriends to keep you busy. And please, call me Giovani." He'd been making this request since she was a girl. "I was sorry to hear about your mother." His words shot through her, seizing her rapidly beating heart. "June was a wonderful woman. I was sad to hear of her passing."

"Thank you." Jillian looked to the ground, observing his scuffed, dirty boots. Giovani had been hard at work, from the stains and scuffs she saw there.

Fresh mulch surrounded them, and there was not a weed to be spotted, not a blade of grass out of place. The Queen's Rose Garden was immaculate. But his words were like a thorn, piercing surprisingly deep.

Giovani Luca believed she was busy. With *friends*.

Popular, even.

If only he knew.

Being 'social' didn't include the five-minute interactions she had at work, taking flower orders, or serving occasional beers at the pub. Real social interaction would include the elusive F word: friends.

I should really contact them.

Adam James and Breanna Henderson, two people who had survived both primary and high school years alongside her, were long overdue for a catchup. 'Adam's Angels' they had called themselves, playing on his massive ego. One teacher had jokingly referred to them as his 'hareem' in high school. *All those years ago...*

At one stage, they had been as close as bees in a hive, but since school had ended, their friendship had waned. The demands of adulting, starting careers and families, all took their toll on their friendship. And losing her mother had made it too hard to face people.

She wasn't ready. She *hadn't been* ready.

Slowly, Jillian was emerging into the world again, willing to delve deeper into people, invest in relationships and connections. *I'll text them tonight*, she vowed, as Giovani's eyes evaluated her.

"It's hard, losing people." Giovani bowed his head respectfully.

"It is." Jillian responded absently, wondering if it was just her mother she'd lost. Somehow, somewhere along the way, she'd lost her mates, and herself, too.

"I think I have something to cheer you up."

The old gardener's hand disappeared into his stained overalls, removing a brown-paper parcel. "I think this is for you. The fellow said a young woman would come to collect it. Someone who loved my work." He smiled proudly as his eyes roamed the garden. "If she were a true admirer of mine, she could be no one else but you, *cara mia*." Giovani chuckled.

"You didn't tell him my name, did you?"

"Course not!" Giovani scoffed. "I wouldn't tell him for all the roses in the world, *bella*. I know you like your privacy. Always have. Even when your mother was here, bless her, you always seemed to prefer to be alone, but with her by your side. That sounds like it doesn't make sense, but–"

Jillian nodded. "Yes, it does," she said, softly.

Giovani's eyes misted as he lost himself in the past.

"Sit together for hours, you and your mum did. Separate people, together. It was lovely to see. Not many can sit in silence and be wholly their own, while belonging to another. Take that bee there." Giovani pointed to the huge buzzing insect nuzzling deep in the centre of a brilliant rose. "He's too busy. He cannot exist in harmony with the flowers. But the butterfly?"

His finger followed the gently looping trail of beautiful orange and black wings. The butterfly settled, calm and still, upon a petal a few feet away.

"She can be still. In sync. Almost become a part of the rose." The old gardener smiled up at Jillian. "You'll find that peace again, *cara mia*. Because you deserve it." Giovani pressed the parcel into her hands. "I'm sorry again for your loss. Pass my best onto your stepfather and sister, if you will. And please, come back soon." He nodded to the flowers. "They miss you."

With a tiny smile of apology, sympathy, or maybe even grandfather-like affection, Giovani nodded once more and left her alone in the sprawling roses.

Tears plucked at her eyes.

The good (and bad) thing about small town life was that almost everyone knew you, your business and your history. Everyone was a relative, or social connection, in some way or another. Nothing could stay hidden for long from the old bush telegram. News spread faster than butter on hot toast, so Jillian was thankful Giovani hadn't given the Mystery Man any information about her. It would have ruined the surprise. This adventure.

Heart in her throat, she tried to swallow her emotions as she sat down heavily on a wooden bench.

Mum ...

Jillian tried to recall her face, her laugh. They slipped further away each day. The heady scent of the roses enticed certain memories, but not the minute details Jillian had been so determined to remember.

It had been one month since her mother passed away. Just four weeks ago. The loneliness and sadness had bored deep into her bones and lingered there. Only a few years earlier, her father had gone. Heart failure. She had scoffed, "what heart?"

Though she had never really known him, the knowledge of his sudden death had settled uneasily in Jillian's mind, filling it with '*what ifs*' and '*if onlys*'. Her stepfather, Wayne, had been the only father figure she actively remembered. Oh, how he had loved June Maitland.

"Jesus, I miss you, Mum," Jillian whispered to the bright, cloudless sky, bringing the brown-paper parcel to her chest. After a few quiet moments, the buzzing of the bees grew louder. The glaring sun began to sting her skin, and Jillian retreated beneath a tall eucalypt. Sinking onto the soft green grass, deliciously cool beneath her, Jillian's hands trembled.

Slowly, she undid the sticky-tape flap on the parcel, smiling as she recognised the forest-green fabric of *Meet Me in Moonshine*. But there was something else in the package. Removing the red note from atop the book, Jillian's eyes scanned D's note.

Dearest J,
I don't mind older women. In fact, I prefer them. The wisdom

of the grey-haired amazes me. They know things us young whippersnappers do not, like the age of the oldest flowers in town.

Honestly, I was shocked when I started to read the plaques Moonshine Council included in the Queen's Rose Garden. So much history in botany. And the smells! Wow!

You're lucky I'm not particularly prone to hay fever. Hold on while I sneeze my nose off...

Jillian found herself laughing at the red note. Laughing! Her Mystery Man had a sense of humour! *Mum would've called him a 'cheeky chops',* she smiled to herself. *One of her favourite traits.* Instantly, her heart lightened with his words.

In honour of your wizened self, I bought you a little gift. Forgive me if the size isn't right.

Excited, and a bit nervous, Jillian removed a white shirt from the package. On the breast pocket, a comic-style woman with grey hair held up a wooden spoon, dripping with pink batter. *Granny May's Bakery* was written in big, bright cursive on the back. D had also left her another blank red paper.

The next Moonshine landmark you should visit sells my favourite food in the entire world. When you get there, I'd like you to guess what it is. If you guess correctly, then this little adventure of ours will continue.

Guess wrong and, well, I suppose you're not the one for me
(is that too presumptuous for our second-blind-date-note?)
Meet me in Moonshine, J. I'm here.
With affection,
D-

With affection ... Butterflies spun in epic loop-the-loops in her stomach. *Get a grip*, she told herself, grinning at the deep red 'Happy Days' roses closest to her.

Meet me ... I'm here. His words spun through her mind.

Despite the heat, a shiver of anticipation ran down her spine.

Thursday

HIDDEN GEM

AFTER AN HOUR DRIVING around town at a snail's pace to read every business banner and sign – occasionally being honked at whilst rolling past – Jillian gave up and ran an internet search for *Granny May's Bakery*. Despite living in Moonshine her entire life, she had never heard of the place.

"Thank God for Google," she told Oscar, scratching him behind the ears. The familiar hum of his purr reverberated through her hand. "It turns out Granny May was one of the pioneer settlers of Moonshine."

Oscar flopped onto one side, the tip of his slinky grey tail flicking to and fro.

"Her bakery is one of Moonshine's oldest shopfronts and is still in operation today! So why don't I know about it?"

Oscar's clear disinterest annoyed her, so Jillian stopped reading aloud.

"You're rude, cat," she grumbled, returning to the website. Moonshinemagic.com told her that despite being rebranded in the 1950s, the name of the original owner, Granny May, had stuck. All the business's promotional merchandise bore a cartoon image of Granny May, based on a grainy photograph supplied by her descendants.

The website also informed Jillian the t-shirt she wore was one of only six produced, as promotional items guaranteeing the wearer free food during February. The shirts had been prizes, won at a charity auction.

Oddly, and encouragingly, the t-shirt fit like a dream.

I wonder if it fits him? *Surely not... The only way this shirt would fit a guy would be if he's prepubescent!* Jillian shuddered at the thought, torn between believing the age of twenty-eight in D's pervious note, or the small size of this t-shirt.

"I just have to trust," she finally realised, speaking to Granny May's printed face, "that what he's written is the truth."

Not only had D given her an exciting puzzle to solve, an excursion, and clothing, he had found a way to shout her a meal as well.

What a charmer. Jillian added 'charming' and 'charitable' to the growing list of heart-fluttering traits she was accumulating about her mysterious local man.

The exact location of Granny May's Bakery surprised Jillian. A true gem, hidden in plain sight, she had driven past that peeling brown door hundreds of times without ever knowing what lay beyond.

The bakery was a small, stone, corner-store building, the kind where the door faced into the middle of the intersection to greet customers from all angles. Shaped like a pentagon, it stretched back into the shopkeeper's home, painted the same creamy white as the shop façade. It was typical of early town planning – business up front, party in the back. Many of Moonshine's businesses were located in (technically zoned) 'residential areas' due to the history of trade and life in colonial times.

A faded blue and white striped awning sheltered two large windows either side of Granny May's antiquated door, featuring an absurdly low brass handle and a mail slot right in the centre. Jillian assumed mail was still inserted through that slit, a daily ritual still observed so many moons after its original construction.

Thinking to the growing collection of red notes in her handbag, Jillian wondered how many letters this door had gobbled throughout its history.

The only indication the place wasn't abandoned was the intoxicating aroma of fresh baked goods seeping out of the very mortar of the building. Having only driven past before, Jillian had never smelled that rich aroma. One deep, delicious breath later, she followed her nose inside.

As her eyes adjusted, Jillian smuggled snorting giggles behind her hand. A few customers turned to look at her, the staff behind the counter openly staring. The mysterious D had wanted her to figure out his favourite food?

Well, it wouldn't be terribly difficult!

The *only* item Granny May's Bakery sold was pie.
Apple, blueberry, blackberry, pineapple and meringue, beef, chicken, curry vegetables, potato ... Every variety of pastry-and-filling combination imaginable was neatly lined up behind the glossy glass counter. *Thank God for small mercies,* she thought, giggling uncontrollably.

He certainly has a sense of humour! Wiping at her eyes, Jillian grappled for control, ducking her head to avoid the strange looks she was collecting.

"Are you okay?" asked a man's silhouette, sitting by one of the large, street-facing windows.

"I'm fine," she spluttered, trying to smother her mirth as she moved to the counter. "Apple pie for me, please," she said, between giggles, to the young girl behind the enticing display.

"Whipped cream or ice-cream?" asked the girl, whose nametag read *Bethany*.

"Both?" Jillian's sweet tooth was working overtime in this place.

"You bet. On the house for one of our winners." Bethany's slim finger pointed to Jillian's shirt. "Take a seat and we'll bring it over."

"Perfect, thank you, Bethany."

There was only one table left, next to the silhouette who had spoken earlier. She watched his back as he stood and strolled to the counter, placing another order. Jillian noticed his shoes. Brown leather Oxfords.

She was still staring at them when he returned to his seat. He smiled, flashing a dimple.

"I was wondering if you'd remember me." One shoe wiggled her way. "Sorry about the other day. I didn't mean to spill your coffee, or my beer." Running a hand through his hair, he laughed.

Jillian's cheeks flushed. "It's no problem, really, it gave me a reason to have a skinny dip in the pool."

Oh, Jesus, did I really just blurt that out?

The thought of this rather attractive man now inevitably imagining her naked and wet caused her stomach to flop dramatically.

"I mean ... I was just ... Oh, Jesus!"

The man roared with laughter, the kind of genuine throw-your-head-back-and-laugh mirth that swept the room up in giggles. He was wiping at his eyes a moment later while Jillian was still marinading in a vat of mortification.

"I'm not good at ... *people*-ing," she admitted quietly, her eyes fixed on his shiny shoes. Who even wore those shoes, anyway? Lawyers? Real estate agents? What did he do for work?

Jillian had spent a lot of time with her head down these past few months. Matching people's shoes to their occupation had become her new favourite game. This man's brown leather business shoes intrigued her. As did his attire.

Today, despite the heat, he was dressed in long pants, a collared shirt and tie. He was well put together. Tailored. Wholesome and clean, he cut a fine figure in his suit, this caffeine-dream-killer.

"Don't worry, I'm not good at being social either," he said, almost conspiratorially. "So, how did you find this place?"

"A friend told me about it." Her eyes flicked to her handbag, where *Meet Me in Moonshine* was safely tucked away, stuffed with red pages, out of sight. Bravely, she raised her eyes to his face.

He nodded, a finger tapping his chin. "Ah, yes. Word of mouth is the only way to get here," he said, standing to leave. "Enjoy your pie." His dimple flashed once more. "And sorry ... again."

She watched his Oxfords move away, the sudden rush of hot summer signalling his departure.

Her apple pie arrived. Granny May's face was etched into the curved end of the custom-made spoon. The waitress slid a coffee onto the table and turned to leave.

"Wait, Bethany! I didn't order this."

"He did." The teenager pointed after the dimples that had just left. "Said he owed you one."

Smiling, Jillian ate the best apple pie of her life, complete with homemade vanilla ice-cream and hand-whipped cream, washing it down with a good (but not as good as Friday's) cappuccino, before sliding the book from her bag.

Dearest D,
Your favourite food is pie? Mince or fruit, minced fruit. Any kind of pie is great! How did you know I adore baked goods?

She faltered, hoping this wouldn't make her sound like a pig.

This shirt won't fit if you send me to any more places like Granny May's!

There. That was better. She'd established the promotional t-shirt was indeed her size, that she was fit, and – what had he written in his previous note? – *the one for me.*

Suddenly, she was too hot. It was too hard to breathe. Her clothing was too tight. Closing her eyes, Jillian forced herself to calm down, imagining she was cool as a cucumber.

Actually, I'll be as cool as Oscar Wild, she corrected, taking a deep breath. Nobody was as chilled and indifferent as that bloody cat.

I think as punishment, I'll have to send you to my favourite place to eat – Moon Shin. Bao and Duyin Shin, the owners, are kind people who cook amazing traditional Chinese food.

Fun fact: many people falsely assume Bao and Duyin misspelled the town's name, when calling their restaurant 'Moon Shin'. The somewhat racist assumption of small-minded people annoys me (hopefully you're not one of them …) In Chinese, 'shin' means 'happy', so the restaurant is essentially the 'happy moon'. I like that. Go there and ask for the 'Jillian special'.

Jesus! Had she just written her name? Oh, no, there it was, on the page. It was too late to turn back now. She only had one red square of paper to write on, and she didn't want to scribble it out ... did she? *Deflect! Move on!*

Here's hoping you don't have any food allergies ...

Jillian paused again, biting her lip, wondering if this was a wise path to travel down. She read the note over, agonising over her stupidity. She hadn't actually said Jillian was her name. *Better sign off quickly, before I do something else completely stupid ..*

Enjoy your meal, oh mysterious local whippersnapper.
Yours,
J-

Yours? Was she his? She barely knew the guy! Yet with every test, every clue, every note, she felt closer to this Mystery Man than she had to anyone else in a long, long time.

Sighing, she thanked Granny May's staff, sliding *Meet Me in Moonshine* across the counter. The young girl winked, moving the novel into a drawer beneath the old-fashioned cash register.

"Thank you," Jillian said. "Someone will collect it from you later."

"Oh, I know. I'm in on the game." Bethany grinned, winking again. "You're lucky, you know," she added, her voice almost a whisper. "He's a catch, your man. It's pretty romantic, how old blue-eyes is organising all these dates for you."

The girl's eyes flicked over Jillian, as though wondering what made her so special. What made her worth such effort.

Wait, old blue eyes? Twenty-eight isn't old! Well, maybe to a fifteen-year-old... Jillian's stomach lurched, and her mouth dropped open as the dots started connecting.

"You know him?"

The girl shrugged, scrunching her nose in a typically noncommittal teenaged manner.

"He's here fairly often. Pretty sure you're wearing his t-shirt right now, though it fits you a lot better." She giggled. "He looked so silly with it tight up around his bellybutton!"

Thank God for that non-teenaged image!

Relief seeped into her tensed muscles. Bethany leaned across the counter, beckoning Jillian closer with a finger.

"Between us girls, are you sleeping with him?"

"WHAT? Jesus, no!"

Bethany shrugged again, looking nonplussed.

"Just asking. You *are* wearing his shirt ..." The implication hang heavily.

"Well, I'm not sleeping with him." *Or anyone.* Jillian groaned inwardly. "I haven't even met him properly, yet. That's part of this 'game'." She used air quotes, repeating the girl's earlier words.

"So, it's like, long-distance blind dating? That's so romantic! Well, I'll keep this here for him. I know he'll call to collect." Then Bethany gushed, "so, can I dish, or what? What can I tell him? I know he'll beg for deets." *Dish. Deets.* Why couldn't teenagers speak English?

Maybe she should drop a hint. She had clues about him, vague as they were.

"Tell him I have dark hair," Jillian said, heading for the door. "And that I loved the apple pie." Then, "wait, can I borrow that back for just a sec?" Jillian located her note and added a PostScript, with Bethany's surprisingly apt labelling of their arrangement rung through her mind.

P.S. Is a long-distance blind date too hopeful? She wrote. **Please leave Meet Me in Moonshine at the Moon Shin restaurant for me to read after my own meal!**

Vowing solemnly to return and sample every pie option in Granny May's Bakery, Jillian turned her thoughts to Moon Shin, wondering how she might explain all this to her aunt.

Friday

MOON SHIN

ALL WEEK JILLIAN HAD watched the waxing moon, feeling the universe building up to something. A moment or important sign, maybe, just in time for February 14th, her impending thirtieth Valentine's birthday. Now, she had involved her aunt and uncle in those universal plans.

"Of course we help!" her aunt, Duyin, had beamed, when Jillian had explained Mystery Man and the scavenger hunt through town.

"Good to see you out of big, lonesome house," added Bao.

Yesterday, Jillian had set the plan in motion, warning a man might soon come to the restaurant, order the Jillian Special and drop a book for her to collect.

"Watch out for him!" Jillian had begged, but Duyin had encouraged her to return tonight, and see for herself. It had seemed smart. Sneaky, but smart. Now, it just felt wrong, lying in wait for a tall man with dark hair, blue eyes and a sense of humour to arrive with the green and gold book.

Bao led Jillian to her usual table. She sat, eyes fixed on the door, set between two wide, circular windows. Beneath the table, her knees bounced. Guilt, embarrassment, shame and anxiety beat upon her brain. Each took their turn, washing over her like waves, while her hot blood hummed with electricity just below the skin's surface.

The energy in her body was creating its own heat. Even the pumping air conditioning of the place couldn't keep her cool.

Duyin poured her a glass of wine.

"Thank you āyí." Jillian nodded thankfully, eyes scanning the customers who entered and left. Moon Shin was getting busy now. It was Friday night, after all.

"Is he here yet?" Duyin asked.

Jillian sighed. "Honestly, I have no idea. He might not even come tonight. Just be on the lookout for the book, okay? He's supposed to leave it here for me to collect."

"Okay, okay, I keep my eyes open." Her aunt offered a small smile, moving quickly to escort more customers to their tables.

Though they weren't blood relatives, Duyin and Bao were the closest to family Jillian and her mother had had in Moonshine.

After her parents' divorce, Jillian and her mother had been regular customers at Moon Shin. They ate there so frequently that, over two decades ago, meals had been named in their honour.

Jillian smiled sadly into her wine glass, gulping deeply as memories forced their way in. For a long time, she'd been suppressing thoughts of her mum. They just hurt too much. Made her absence too real. Now, she couldn't escape them. They rose like the bubbles in soda, millions of moments caught in the glass of her life.

June Maitland had been a terrible cook. As much as Jillian had loved her mother, it was a truth universally acknowledged that June's culinary skills had more holes than Ned Kelly's armour. The first, second, tenth ... twentieth time they had stumbled through the restaurant's doors, dinner had been inedible charcoal.

The only restaurant still open, warm and welcoming, Moon Shin became a version of home that didn't smell like a bushfire.

June had been blessed to meet Wayne. Jillian's stepfather was a decent cook; the kind of home-style chef who swore by the meat-and-three-vegetables rule. He loved firing up the barbeque, or baked huge hunks of meat, served with veggies, always.

Wayne happily indulged in the occasional meal 'on the town' at Moon Shin, respecting Jillian's adopted aunt and uncle as extended family. It was probably one of the reasons she had learned to love him so quickly.

Tonight, for the first time, being here felt wrong. Spying wasn't part of the rules. There weren't rules to this game, *technically*, but still, she was breaking the unwritten code.

"This is wrong."

Bao floated closer. "Jillian, you okay?"

"I have to go. Sorry, Bao. Tell Duyin I'll visit again soon."

Rising to leave, she considered how many rules she had broken. She had written her name! She was attempting to spy, to catch out her Mystery Man, to wreck this game and bend the rules of the scavenger hunt! He wouldn't have done that. He would've been better ... right?

A mishmash of images from each of the places in Moonshine she had visited collided in her mind. Had he been there? Had *he* been spying on *her*? How would she even know? Her eyes flew around the restaurant before landing on the till.

Meet Me in Moonshine was leaning casually, propped beside a pile of menus by the lucky cat statue.

He's here!

The sight of the book sent fresh waves of guilt through her. It pooled in her stomach, a hot, knotting weight. She swerved around an old couple clinking glasses merrily, feet carrying her towards the door.

"Such. An. Idiot." Jillian berated herself.

Just grab the book and go.

She attempted to dodge a woman fanning out her blonde hair, trying to cool her neck in the air-conditioning. A lock of hair flicked in Jillian's face, stabbing like a needle in her eye. As she cried out, the large party turned to look at her. Their open-mouthed faces blurred as pain and tears muddled her sight.

"Oh, come on!" Jillian muttered to the universe, frustrated. It was punishing her, she knew. She stumbled backwards, her hand over her eye, arse bumping into the edge of a table.

Losing her balance, Jillian dropped heavily into a chair. No, not a chair. It was warm and firm. *Someone's lap!?*

"I'm so sorry," she told the person-chair, trying to make out the figure through her watering eyes.

"Woah there, Daisy. You okay?" A familiar voice filtered through and she felt herself sliding sideways. Two large, warm hands grabbed her waist, holding her steady.

"Um – yes?"

Daisy? Only one person, maybe two, was able to get away with calling her that.

The person laughed, then spoke again.

"Way to make an entrance, girl. Oops. Here – let me fix your dress, Dais."

A hand tugged at her waist, adjusting fabric. Oh, Jesus, had she just flashed the entire restaurant?

Daisy ... It had to be him. *It has to be.*

"Adam?"

A warm hand grabbed hers and squeezed. "Yeah, babe, it's me. You okay there, Daisy Duke?"

Jillian melted into Adam, laughing with relief. Of all people, it had to be him. *Thank Heavens for small miracles.*

"You'll never forgive me for those denim shorts, will you?"

"No, I'll never *forget* those *tiiiiiny* denim shorts. There's a difference."

"If you got it–" she sighed as he laughed.

"Flaunt it, Dais. But no more flashing your knickers around to everyone, okay? I mean, I know I'm a handsome guy, but here isn't the place for exposed panties ..."

Jillian's face flushed.

Despite his bad reputation, she considered Adam an angel. Jillian could never understand why the town saw him in any other way than she did. Sure, she could admit that it was hard to see beyond his exterior. The dude *was* an Adonis, if you liked smooth-skinned, underwear-model-like looks.

Adam had often been described around town as 'sex on legs', but that didn't mean he was a *bad guy*. At least, he'd never given her that impression.

In all their years of friendship (yes, she could still call it that, despite their recent distance), Adam had always been there. Like now. He'd caught her. Her chair-man hero who'd hidden her pink floral panties from Moon Shin's diners.

Leaning back against Adam's chest, Jillian swiped tears from her eyes. Beneath her, Adam's body stiffened and his two strong arms circled her waist, clasping her lightly. He squeezed her hand.

Wait, what? Adam was still holding her hand! But there were two arms around her? Had he grown another arm?
How could he...

Blinking furiously, she swivelled to examine the man whose lap she was perched on. It wasn't Adam. Adam was standing next to chair-man, his eyes wide and full of concern.

The human seat beneath her had blue eyes and, *oh Jesus*, a very cute and *familiar* set of dimples.

Jillian jumped up from the Coffee-Killer's lap, forcing Adam to take a step backwards as she buried her head in his chest. Smoothing her hair, he murmured sweet things like, "Don't drop your petals all at once, Daisy. Chin up, love," while she mumbled embarrassed apologies to everyone in earshot, avoiding all eye contact.

It wasn't the first time Adam had consoled her and, aware of her tendency for embarrassment and leaking eyes, it wouldn't be the last, either.

This is exactly why it's easier to be alone. Jillian sniffled. *You can't mess up anyone else's life when you're flying solo.*

"I'm just leaving," she told Adam's table, smoothing down her dress. Adam stroked her arm, calming her, smiling his way-too-photogenic smile. Their entire *ten-person* table stared back at her, revelling in her awkward moment.

Oh, God, no ...

Her mortification level blew its top. It was summer in Australia, already a million degrees, but she may as well have been camping on the surface of the sun right now.

If spontaneous combustion was a real thing, Jillian Maitland would be the next to burst into flames.

Get the extinguishers ready, Bao.

Attempting retreat was useless. Adam's hand still grasped hers. *Looks like we're burning together then, buddy.*

"Can't stay away, hey?" Dimples smiled up from his seat, cheeks flushed.

He looked different tonight. Gone were the professional suit and leather shoes. In a collared white shirt, jeans, and steel-capped work boots, he may as well have just stepped off the set of the latest hit reality renovation TV show. A show with a cast of super-fit people, like soccer players or gym junkies or something.

What do you do for work? She wondered again, eyes flicking between him and Adam, searching for their connection.

Speaking of gym junkies ...

Adam had clearly come straight from work. His business logo for 'Fit But' – a fist raised powerfully and holding a hand weight – was embroidered on his chest. Was this some kind of 'cheat meal' convention for his fitness clients?

Looking around the table, Jillian noted the mix of men and

women, professional and casual. Each was in their twenties or thirties; some of the men dark haired and blue eyed. She turned towards the cash register. *Meet Me in Moonshine!*

He's here! He's still *here!* The book, this adventure, was messing with her mind.

Wide-eyed, she looked to Adam. Deep, ocean-eyed, black-haired Adam.

No! It can't be! Can it?

"Do you want to have dinner with us?" Dimples interrupted her mental spiral. "One of our friends bailed, so there's room at the table." Jillian looked to the pint-spilling Coffee-Killer. Who had baby blue eyes and dark brown hair.

Oh, no.

Jillian's eyes reassessed the party once more.

Oh, Jesus, no!

Three of the men at the table could have been described as tall, with blue eyes and dark hair.

But then ... disappointment and frustration tightened the knot in her gut. Multiply the men at this table by *all* the tables in *Moon Shin*, and she had a rather large pool of potentials who might be her Mystery Man. Too large. Jillian swayed unsteadily, overwhelmed.

"Dais, I think you'd better sit down, love." Adam guided her to a chair. A real chair, not a man's lap. "She'll have a glass of wine and the Jillian Special," Adam told Bao, who nodded and zipped away.

That's it! The Jillian Special! With any luck, I'll be able to narrow down the search for my Mystery Man by his order! A flicker of guilty, nervous hope reignited.

Ten minutes later, Jillian was pushing chunks of chicken around her plate, watching it stick to the fluffy rice, hopelessness rising. Seven of ten people at the table had ordered the Jillian Special. Throughout the entire restaurant, this order seemed too damn common for Jillian's current tastes.

"This is delicious," Adam moaned through a mouthful. "It's better than sex … *almost.*" He grinned wolfishly. All the women nodded agreement, fluttering their eyelashes at him.

"Always great food here at Moon Shin," a dark-haired, blue-eyed man named Charlie said.

Maybe it's him? She dared to wonder.

He continued, "I wonder why they didn't spell the name of this place properly?"

Nope, you're not him. Can't be.

"So, Daisy, is it?" one of the women purred, leaning across

Adam, just far enough for her breasts to brush his arm. It was a predatory move. She was claiming him. Completely unnecessarily, but the calculated flirtation prickled like a grass seed against Jillian's skin.

If you were a cat, she thought, *you'd be just like Oscar, sneaking into bedrooms at night.*

"How do you know Adam?" Cat asked.

Jillian shovelled food into her mouth to avoid answering.

Adam winked.

"Ooh, like *that* is it?" Cat purred.

No! Jillian wanted to scream. *It's not like that at all!*

"How long have you been ..." Cat paused purposefully, "*friends*?"

Jillian nearly choked.

"Since childhood, hey Dais?" Adam threw an arm around her shoulder, grinning around the table. "This chick's golden, I tell you. *Golden.* One of a kind. And her sister's a bit of all right, too."

Jillian's cheeks flamed. Adam turned to her, oblivious to the implications he was sending out to his friends.

"We should hook up ..." Adam paused to swallow his mouthful, insinuation filling his silence. "... more regularly, though," he finished. *There you go with the innuendo again,* she inwardly moaned, watching Cat's face turn steely, the green-eyed monster flashing in her eyes.

"Only teenagers say 'hook up'," Jillian said to lighten the mood. Despite using the wrong words, she had to concede his message was correct. Adam was right, it had been too long since they'd had a proper catch up.

"And yes," she agreed, swallowing hard. "We should."

Cat's eyes bore down on Jillian. *If looks could kill* ... Eating faster, she tried to avoid conversation. Turns out, all rapid consumption ensures is a healthy dose of indigestion and sitting awkwardly, watching everyone else chewing.

It was already awkward enough, but now she had to find something else, something that wasn't mastication, to stare at. The weave of the white linen tablecloth suddenly became very interesting. Hot-cheeked, Jillian folded her hands in her lap, trying not to compare herself to the other women, who delicately mouthed ridiculously tiny portions at a time.

Just great. Another strike in the Can't Function in Society tally.

"I like a woman who can eat," another blue-eyed, dark-haired fellow said, drawing her gaze up. This one had a man bun and light stubble stretching its way across his wide, smiling mouth.

He had an intriguing face. Gentle, yet angular. His background was clearly Southern European, with curling dark hair and tanned olive skin. Crow's feet sprung from the corners of his dark-lashed eyes, the kind that spoke of long summers in the sun and dependable laughter.

Jillian just knew that beneath the table, he'd be wearing those chunky Birkenstock sandals she whole-heartedly believed should be outlawed when worn with socks.

Why wear socks and sandals, anyway?

She would never understand people who made such a fashion faux pas. Would footwear be a deal breaker if this rather handsome Man-Bun man, who was currently finishing his Jillian Special, turned out to be her mystery Moonshine date?

"I like to eat." Jillian shrugged at him, offering a shy smile. "And the food here is great."

"Do you come here often?" another person asked her.

"I do, actually."

"Would you like a coffee, since you've finished your meal?" Dimples asked.

"Yes, please. Just a half-strength cappuccino with a shot of vanilla and extra chocolate dusting." She didn't feel like adding the cinnamon tonight, or her usual jet-fuel strength caffeine injection.

The Coffee-Killer laughed. "*Just*? That's one heck of an order. Is that what you spilled on me?"

Jillian balked. "You spilled your *disgusting* beer and my *amazing* coffee onto *me*, if I remember correctly. So you owe me, Coffee-Killer."

"Ouch, straight to the heart." Clutching his chest, he smirked, a dimple winking into existence. "Don't forget, I've already paid back the spilled coffee. You still owe me a beer, though." He cocked an eyebrow, dimples deepening as he stood and strode to the counter, where Duyin was already making an order of hot beverages.

The night was winding down, diners enjoying the remnants of their meals. It was kind of him to make it right, shouting her a coffee. It wouldn't be as good as Friday's Café (nothing was) but it was a sip in the right direction.

Buying Dimples a pay-back beer wouldn't be so easy. A woman buying a man a drink at the bar could be misconstrued as liquid flirtation, unless she bought a round for the group.

"So, Daisy Duke." Adam grinned at her, beer on his breath as he leaned close. Too close, but he was like that. He dipped his head, accentuating his deep, ocean-blue, puppy-dog eyes. "Wanna come dancing, love? Shake your groove thing with me? Twerk? Bump and grind? We could do that power lift from

Dirty Dancing. What do you say?" Adam flicked her upper thigh playfully, causing her to squeal.

"I don't know, Adam," Jillian checked her watch. "I'm not my own boss, unlike some." She nudged him in the ribs. "I'm supposed to work tomorrow."

"What do you do for work?" Man-Bun asked, leaning forward, like he was genuinely interested.

"I'm a florist."

Everyone (except the green-eyed Cat) nodded like she'd said something really important.

"So, what say you?" Adam slid his hand around her waist. "You still owe me a dance from our high school graduation. I still can't believe I couldn't find you that night. I think you must've taken off with your sister by then." He winked. "They were always giving me the slip! But not tonight, love. Tonight we pay our debts."

"Speaking of debts, she owes me a beer," Dimples put in, setting a full white mug of heavenly coffee before her.

Jillian glared at them. "I do *not* –" she pointed finger, settling on one and then the other, "owe either of you anything."

Man-Bun laughed. "I'd take a beer, if you're offering to buy the first round?"

Be careful what you wish for, Jillian!

Sighing, she finally relented.

"Okay," she said to cheers around the table. "Just *one* dance and *one* round of beers, though."

Saturday

Home is Where the Heart Aches

"Oscar Wild," Jillian moaned, "you, sir, are an arsehole."

He'd stolen the bed. The entire bed! How a small cat could refuse to give her room on the big bed was a mystery. Oscar had contentedly purred the night away while she'd slept on the couch. It was old and lumpy-cushioned, with stabbing, squeaky springs.

I would have slept better on the floor. At least the tiles would be cool, unlike Oscar. The cat was a furry furnace of a creature. A furnace she wanted to avoid right now. She was already burning with regret.

Her head hurt.

Her feet throbbed.

Her cheeks ached.

Her heart thumped too heavily and, strangely, in her temples. And last night's dress was kicked up indelicately around her waist.

But despite this glorious, lady-like awakening, as she lunged to the toilet and curled around its bowl, Jillian couldn't remember the last time she'd had *that* much fun.

Why didn't she laugh that much all the time? She'd been light as a balloon and just as fit to burst.

When had she last danced like that, with total abandon? To ignore what people thought, what she looked like? When had she last just let loose?

Loose... she pondered the word. That's exactly how she felt. Like a huge knot that was slowly coming undone, tension releasing, the awful tightness becoming less constrictive.

Breathe... she thought. *I feel like I can breathe again ...*

At the beginning of the night, she had made a meticulous study of shoes. They really revealed a lot about people, and recently, she'd taken to examining fabric, size, colour, laces and soles, to avoid eye contact.

No longer.

No more shambling zombie. She was a *hot zombie*. A recovering shuffler who was learning to walk again, like that movie, *Warm Bodies*.

Last night had been a revelation. A return to the Jillian of years past. Somehow, in all the spinning and laughing and drinking (*oh God, the drinking*) Adam and his friends had peeled back her hard exoskeleton to reveal the shiny, fresh person she really was. The version of Jillian who had been hiding within her own skin.

Literally shaking off her worries last night, she had made the biggest change yet – she had simply had *fun*. Fun with new friends, like Man-Bun, whose default characteristic was chuckling and curling stray tendrils of hair behind his ear.

And that Charlie guy, the one she wrote off. He wasn't her mystery note writer, but he danced like nobody was watching, dragging others into his crazy, elaborate routines.

Magnetic and entertaining, he had whirled anyone (and everyone) around the dance floor, dragging people into the conga, leading the crowd, and reminding them how to line-dance to 'The Nutbush'. Hell, he'd even known the moves to 'The Macarena' and the Spice Girls' 'Stop'! Charlie was the reason her feet were screaming and begging for amputation right now.

Jillian wasn't sure why she was so shocked by the evening. A night with Adam James promised fun, no matter who else was there. *He's always been a guaranteed good time.*

Pride swelled within her. Reconnecting with Adam had been a great idea, despite it causing a level of uncomfortable social pain.

It's his beautiful face ... and all the abs. And those biceps! Why he'd chosen to open a gym rather than grace the cover of every magazine in the universe, Jillian couldn't understand. The guy could make millions overnight if he started an 'Only Fans' account, and he knew it. He oozed sex appeal like other men secreted sweat.

Adam played it up, in fact. He liked to touch, to pinch or stroke, and he spoke in a litany of double entendre that could infuriate people. People like her sister, who refused to see him as anything other than an immature child. A callous heartbreaker who only thought with his dick. His devastatingly good looks were his burden to bear, but last night, Jillian had somehow worn it, too.

Ridiculously pretty, sexually predatory women had given her the stink eye all evening. She'd noticed early on, and tried to ignore it, but ultimately it grated on her comfort in the group. Just thinking about their judging looks settled a chill in her bones.

He's all yours, she'd wanted to scream at them last night. *Don't hate the player, hate the game! I'm NOT here to play! I am not your competition!*

She understood why anyone with ovaries might have been jealous. After habitually flirting with numerous women all evening, Adam and Jillian had left the dance floor (and then the bar) together last night. To envious onlookers, it had indicated only one thing. One thing she'd absolutely promised herself years ago she would never do with Adam.

Sex.

Jillian wouldn't deny she'd considered it ... rather a lot, in fact. She was only human, after all.

But this wasn't a line in the sand. It was a boundary set in concrete. She would never break a promise to her sister who, long ago, made Jillian swear a blood oath to stay romantically detached from Adam James.

Last night, Jillian had replayed that memory on repeat as she and Adam giggled and reminisced the entire ten-minute walk to her home on Farthing Street. Adam gallantly escorted her 'for safety'.

It wasn't necessary. Moonshine was a safe place. A clean place. The kind of town that won awards for tidy streets and unusually low crime levels. Even in the dead of night, Moonshine's dark alleys screamed 'old world charm' rather than 'serial killer lurking in the shadows'.

Blowing kisses and wondering aloud if he could climb the drainpipe, like he had in their school years, Adam had stepped back from her front door, appraising the latticework.

"Don't you dare!" Jillian had called after his retreating shadow. "Oscar will kill you! My bedroom's his territory."

Adam had thrown his hands up, laughing. "I'm not one to go cutting someone else's lunch!"

Jillian laughed. "Who even says that, Adam? Women aren't snacks, you know!" She blushed, suddenly realising the weight of possible connotations.

"I respectfully disagree. But you know what I mean, Dais," his white-toothed grin lit up the night. "I'm not in the business of stealing another man's woman. Hell, the last time I *tried* ..." He chuckled, "well, let's just say it didn't go so well."

Adam sauntered off down the street, his hands shoved in his pockets. Briefly, he turned. "Hey, Dais?"

"Yes?" she called into the darkness.

"I'm really sorry about your mum. She was ..."

"Yeah, I know. She was great. Thank you, Adam. Goodnight."

Fumbling with the sharp-edged shadows that were her keys, Jillian had eventually seen herself in the front door, and didn't remember much beyond that point.

Now, rising on aching feet from the bathroom floor, she wobbled her way into the living room. Memories rose and fell like waves – last night, last week, years ago – all crashing together.

"Yep, the single women of Moonshine would've given anything for him to walk them home," she told one of the neatly lined Maitland family photos on the mantelpiece.

The date stamp was hidden behind the frame, but she knew exactly when this photo had been taken – the year her father abandoned them. Sometimes she worried about how she could like Adam but hate her father, when they possessed similar, spectacularly high girlfriend tallies.

Those women would have *begged* Adam into their bedrooms, Jillian was sure. Had it been the same for her dad? Couldn't see the forest for the trees?

Jillian's stepfather and his daughter, her sister from another mister, grinned out from the next photo. "That was the year we all made a new family," she advised the photograph, as though it needed reminding.

In the image, her youthful self held a tight grip on her new sister's hand, their eyes drifting toward each other, caught up in the excitement.

It had been a progressive, bold move to become one of the first blended families in Moonshine – a town where marriage lasted longer than most prison sentences.

Jillian gently touched the frame. *I should really go see them ...*

Younger versions of more school friends, Breanna Henderson and Billy Carmichael, alongside Adam James and herself, grinned from the next photo.

The image depicted New Year's Eve, 1999.

Jillian couldn't quite remember how old they had been. What she did recall was the sheer panic of the world.

Everyone had feared the 'millennium bug' that was about to fry technology and reset modern civilisation when the clock struck midnight. Their little posse had celebrated by spending a night by candlelight, wearing tinfoil hats.

Even then, Adam had been heart-achingly gorgeous. If she remembered correctly, he'd also been deeply sad. Dismissing it as typical New Year's Eve Blues had been easy when he had admitted to feeling rather lonely ... especially with no one to kiss at midnight.

"We're all here!" Bre had laughed. "Any of us will kiss you!"

"Not me!" Billy and Jillian said simultaneously, bursting into laughter as a sour look bloomed on Adam's face.

"I'm too young for kissing anyways!" Jillian always had been a late bloomer. Not that maturity mattered much among the youth of Moonshine.

In a small town where school grades were a convoluted and composite mess of kids, age had never really factored into life. Not then, anyways. As her thirtieth birthday rapidly approached, age certainly felt like it weighed in a lot more *now*.

"But it's just not the same." Adam had sighed as fireworks lit up the night.

She had waited for the tell-tale wink, the wolfish grin that meant he'd been fishing for compliments and playing with them, but it never came. And however old they'd been, Jillian remembered thinking how he had seemed so much older in that moment.

Not for the first time, she wondered if Adam James was her Mystery Man. How would it affect their long-term friendship? If he was the note writer, a jackhammer might be readily taken to that concrete boundary she'd carefully laid years ago. The person she was *then* was not who she was *now*. Maybe this new phase of life could be a new phase with him, too?

But the note writer had said he was *lonely* ...

Adam James didn't seem lonely. Not now, at least. He was always surrounded by people. Always laughing. But Jillian knew that 'lonely' wasn't a mask people wore on the outside. Even a crowded room couldn't eclipse Jillian's feelings of isolation, recently.

Only time might tell who her Mystery Man was, *if* her note writer ever revealed himself. This scavenger hunt could last years, if the aim was to explore Moonshine's hidden gems.

Jillian considered her home one such gem, though inviting her Mystery Man to explore her rooms was light years away from reality.

Absently, her fingers brushed the low brass doorknobs of the hallway doors as she padded further away from the bathroom. Her fingers skating up the smooth, wooden banister of the staircase, she climbed the familiar path to her bedroom, avoiding the creaky steps with practiced care.

She hadn't made it this far last night, falling on the couch just a few steps inside the front door. Aching feet and a curdling stomach hadn't allowed her to trek much further.

As it was, each footstep felt like walking on needles that pushed all the way to her ankles. But oh, the dancing! Jillian wouldn't trade last night for the world.

Sunlight streamed in through the stained-glass windows, casting a bright, almost mystical light. The organ in her chest thumped low and hard as she reached the landing, where two massive bedrooms split off on either side: hers, and her mother's. That second door remained shut.

Home might be where the heart is, but it's also where it has free rein to ache in the deepest and most familiar of recesses.

Jillian had basked in her broken-ness for too long; wallowing in self-pity and sadness, repressed guilt and grief.

This big, empty house, full of echoes had gobbled her up. It was a beautiful monster, her home. With its ceiling roses and chandeliers, wainscotting, open fireplaces, and unique, ornamental cornices, the 'Maitland Mansion' had been her mother's project. Her second baby.

Jillian's parents had purchased the house on Farthing Street as a restoration project, aiming to rent out each stately room as part of a heritage B&B. But when her father left, the funds were sucked up in the divorce settlement. The house, huge and demanding, fell into disrepair.

Until, that is, they had met Wayne West. Injecting time, care, and patience with both the project (and the two new women in his life) he had been the best stepfather anyone could have gifted to Jillian, and an adoring husband for her mother.

A local builder, Wayne was what her mother, June, had called 'as rare as hen's teeth,' and 'the kind of man you should marry, Jilly'.

Wayne had painstakingly breathed new life into the polished floorboards and paintwork, but that was years ago. Echoes of June's delighted laughter and pride in his attention still rung through the railings.

Now, the house was still beautiful, but more in a 'haunted

house' or 'quaint antiques museum' manner. Jillian loved the old home, but it was full of ghosts and echoes that filled her with sudden melancholy if she stayed here too long alone. Left with only her thoughts, the sadness crept back in.

Keeping busy was key and having energy for all that required caffeine. *Strong Coffee = Stay Awake and Busy = No Time To Dwell.*

Oscar came slinking out of her room, rubbing himself along the ledge of the windows, silver fur dappled in bright colourful streaks.

"No more," she told him. "I can't be that introverted person anymore. Don't let me, okay?" Her furry boyfriend arched his shiny spine into her. "I had such a great night, unexpected as it was," she told him. "And today I feel … different. More present, I think. I'm dead tired, but that's just in my body, not in my heart, you know?"

Oscar flicked his grey tail, swayed his butt and, indifferent to her outpouring of emotion and ground-breaking personal realisations, slipped out the window.

Newton Falkner's 'Gone in the Morning' started playing on the radio and Jillian couldn't help but smile. *Oh, the irony.*

Normally her alarm would be dragging her from bed at this hour, but for now, she'd turn it off and rest, a happy weariness weighing her down.

"Meet you in Moonshine," she sleepily mumbled out the window, as Oscar's slinky body snuck over the high fence. "See you tonight."

At 5pm, Jillian jolted awake. Sliding her phone closer, she auto-dialled, heart racing.

"Hello, Moon Shin. What you want to order?"

"Duyin, āyí, it's Jillian."

"Oh, hello Jillian, baby girl, how you today? Head hurt?"

Her self-adopted aunt cackled.

"Yes. But that's not why I'm calling. Is the book there?"

Duyin went silent.

"Aunt? Āyí, are you there?"

"So sorry, baby girl. No green and gold book here."

"Oh." Her heart sunk through her stomach lining and fell out her butt. *It* had *been there ... right?*

"Want me call when book arrive?"

"Yes, please, āyí. Thank you."

"Okay, bye bye."

It was only then she saw a text message from Iris Bloom.

> Jillian, honey, are you ok? You missed
> your shift and I'm a bit worried …

"Oh, Jesus," she moaned, quickly firing off a reply:

> I am so sorry, Iris. I should have text you.
> I'm not feeling myself. Talk soon x

Sunday

PROGRESS ON PAUSE

9am.
Calls: 0. Voicemail: 0. 1 instant coffee (and many instant regrets, but Friday's was closed one Sunday a month and today happened to be that one bloody day).

10:20am.
Magazines: 2. Calls from Moon Shin: 0

12:02pm.
1 sandwich. 1 more instant coffee. 0 missed calls. 1 big ball of anxiety knotted in Jillian's gut.

1:47pm.
Calls to Moon Shin Chinese Restaurant: 2. Brisk discussions with Bao: 2. Apologies: numerous.

3:38pm.

Jillian checked her phone, opening a text chain with Adam James.

> Hey you. Thanks again for Friday night. I had a really good time. We should do it again, soon. Missing you!

> Sup Daisy! It was gr8 to see u out n about, back in the land of the living. You're like some hot zombie chick who's just been rezurected.
> I know that's spelt wrong. So sue me.

> I didn't go 2 class much back in school if u remember. 2 busy with … uh … physical education ;P

Then, in quick succession, Adam sent each single thought as a separate text.

> Wotevz. Point is that I'm so proud of u babe!

> I 4got u had such sweet dance flore mooves.

> My m8s were impressed!

My head is killing meeeee.

Sorry about the Sambuca. My bad. Talk soon.

LOL you can count on it. Rest up x

6:32pm.

Netflix: Are you still watching? Calls from Moon Shin: 0. Calls to Moon Shin: 2. Times lectured by Duyin: 1. Times briskly told "not to tie up the business line for personal matters even though we love you dearly" by Bao: 1.

By 7:04pm, Jillian's phone is stuffed between the lounge cushions and one furry boyfriend is making for an excellent distraction.

Oscar, apparently impervious to the stifling summer heat, was snuggled in the very centre of Jillian's bed.

Unable to sleep in the belly of an active volcano, and with an overactive, anxiety-riddled brain, Jillian slipped outside, her feet plodding of their own accord towards the pool. The surface shimmered and rippled lightly as tiny bugs dipped their toes into the water.

The moon was brilliant, full of promise.

Milky, silvery light gently kissed everything it touched. The Man in the Moon smiled warmly down on her as she slipped off her light cotton nightie and slid into the water, sighing.

Why didn't I do this earlier? The water always washed away her woes.

"This is ridiculous," she told the Milky Way, imagining her mother was up there, one of the many millions of stars that were tuned in, listening, and shining just for her tonight.

"I can't be this obsessed about a boy. A boy I don't even know. Not really. Well, a *man*. He is twenty-eight, after all ... hopefully."

She sighed again, thinking the stars probably gave exactly zero shits about the semantics of the mysterious D's age.

"All I really know is he's tall, dark ... and handsome, I bet. With brilliant sapphire eyes and a sense of humour, and a deep and warm laugh, showing his dimples."

Dimples? Wait, where did that come from?

Images of the caffeine-killing pint spiller hit her like a wrecking ball. His work boots shuffling alongside Adam's trainers and her sandals on the dance floor. Long, heavy looks across the beer-soaked bar and somewhat intense, up-close conversations. Laughter. *Dear Jesus, so much laughter*. Her cheeks ached at the memory.

"What an unexpected night." She smiled up to the inky sky.

Wait, did she *like* Dimples? But the equally cute, equally dark-haired and blue-eyed Man-Bun had been there too. Buying her drinks, grinding on the dance floor, laughing alongside her, running his hand through his hair. He had been overflowing with compliments and conversation, making her feel interesting ... and *alive*.

"Oh, Jesus, what was his *name*?" She was sure Adam had said it. All night she'd teasingly called them Coffee-Killer (or Dimples), and Man-Bun. Following Adam's lead, the group had called her Daisy. No real names exchanged, to her memory, which, admittedly, was extremely hazy and rather waterlogged.

Both men had left an impression, but somehow, her fantasy fellow had acquired dimples. It was telling.

Jillian remembered the Coffee-Killer's soft touch, the warm callouses on his hands. Did he work with those hands? She imagined all the things he might do with his warm digits.

Taking a quick look around the pool, knowing full well she was out of sight from everyone but Oscar and the odd passing fruit bat, she grinned slyly to herself. She was invisible right now.

Good.

Her hands began a slow, slippery descent through the water as she imagined tracing the indent of his cheeks with her fingers. Slowly, she slid her hands over her body, ripples of anticipation lapping at her. Goosebumps tingling all over, Jillian slowly dipped her fingertips down, pressing lightly in exactly the right spot when it reached the small thatch of dark hair between her legs.

When did I last do this? she asked herself, her head tipping back as a powerful, heavy urge thrilled her.

Wait, is this considered cheating?

On my sort-of-almost-maybe-a-boyfriend non-boyfriend?

Mortified by the thought, her hands flew to the water's surface.

"Am I a *cheater*?"

Putting Dimples (and, let's be honest, Man-Bun too) into the spank bank and imagining how he might employ his hands wasn't being *unfaithful* to her Moonshine scavenger-hunt Mystery Man ... right?

Jillian pushed both hands to the cold tiles lining the pool's edge, breathing hard.

"Oh, Jesus, what am I going to do?" she asked the bats, mere shadows in the night. The mysterious D, the self-confessed 'lonely' man who had intrigued her all week, who'd gotten her out of her comfort zone and into the world; the guy who had made her laugh and feel alive again. Ultimately, he was a very tangible man. One she very much wanted to meet, eventually.

But Dimples ... Well, he was a clumsy jerk who kept showing up at the most random of times, but he'd been sweet in repaying her for the spilled coffee incident and had been there to pick her up, quite literally, as she stumbled through life recently. She knew his face and his friends, who were also her friends now.

Thanks, Sambuca. She groaned.

Dimples was handsome and he smelled like David Beckham (she knew, because she'd asked while they were dancing 'The Nutbush'). Importantly, he wasn't just a slip of paper. He was a full-flesh-and-blood man, and he was *here*.

"It's all your fault, Dad, you jerk. You've completely messed up my ideas about men."

Oscar meowed from high above, pushing the bedroom window open further. He must have finally realised how hot a second-storey bedroom became in high summer. Oscar Wild. The one fellow who hadn't just snuck into her heart, but also into her bedroom.

Sighing deeply, Jillian tried to resume her previous activity, to no avail. She would spend the next hour in the pool, overthinking her predicament, pondering men, relationships, love letters, and being what Adam called a 'hot zombie'.

Unwilling to towel off because she'd be mostly dry by the time she reached the house anyway, *damn Australian summer*, Jillian staggered back to bed. She toppled, mentally exhausted and still damp, into immediate sleep beside Oscar.

The cat shifted uncomfortably on Jillian's bed, staring in annoyance at Jillian's phone as an incoming call from Moon Shin vibrated his crisp cotton sheets.

Monday

DISCONNECT TO RECONNECT

JILLIAN LEFT HER SWIFT at home and ran to Moon Shin. It had been a while since she'd bothered with the stretchy activewear and her old trainers, but her usual cotton summer dresses weren't made for the new land speed record she was about to set. Running wasn't her thing, usually. Her stepsister jogged daily, but it had never appealed to Jillian. Until today, that is.

Panting, heart about to explode from her chest and sweat pooling in her bra, Jillian burst through the restaurant doors ... and right into *him*. One of the objects of her dreams. Someone who, in spirit at least, had been fondling her in the pool last night.

"Woah! Hold on there, Daisy!" Man-Bun's smiling eyes greeted her with their familiar warmth. He reached out, steadying her as she reeled back from his broad chest.

Her hands found his arms, though whether she was trying to steady her feet or her hormones, she wasn't sure.

Jesus, he's stunning!

He was so hot he may as well have been the sun itself. You could bask in his light and walk away with a tan.

"Man-Bun!" The blurted nickname tickled his fancy. Those blue eyes crinkled further, almost disappearing as he burst into laughter. It was soft and light, not the boom of Dimple's laugh, but still pleasant and contagious.

"What are you doing here?" Jillian giggled nervously.

Are you him? Did Meet Me in Moonshine *just leave your hands to make their way into mine?*

He tucked a stray tendril of his long, dark brown hair behind one ear, smiling down at her.

"Forgot something. Well, technically I *lost* it. But it was here all along." He curled his long hair behind one ear before shoving his hands into his pockets. Presumably to fondle said item, as he didn't produce any other explanation or evidence. "Well, better be off. Got a big day at the office." He whistled, rolling his eyes and grinning.

Jillian looked down at his shoes. Yep, they were office appropriate leather shoes, not the socks-and-sandals combo she'd fretted over. *Thank God.*

"See you around?" Man-Bun asked, hope thick in his tone.

"Definitely. That would be great." Jillian smiled up at him as a yell came through the restaurant.

"FINALLY!"

Man-Bun's eyebrow rose as he spied Duyin racing towards the door. The door they were now blocking. *He* was blocking, more accurately, with his 'Clearly I Love Exercise' muscular frame. Jillian couldn't block a lamp post on a good day.

Jillian grimaced, pointing toward Duyin. "That's my cue."

"Oooookay. Well, bye." Man-Bun gave her arm a little squeeze as he slipped past her and into the street. "I look forward to the next time we bump into each other," he said over his shoulder as the door jangled shut behind him. Jillian's heart did that weird flip-flop of hope and excitement.

"FINALLY!" Duyin huffed again, practically throwing *Meet Me in Moonshine* at her, grinning widely. "Here your book."

"Āyi. Thank you." Jillian plonked down in the nearest seat, ignoring the small 'reserved' sign and gulping water from the glass set before her. Flicking through the pages, she scanned for a tell-tale red paper.

Heart growing heavy, stomach lurching, she flicked through the entire thing.

Every. Last. Page.

No note.

No, wait! Peeling back the dust jacket, she found her prize. With a little squeal, Jillian pressed it to her chest.

"You know," Duyin commented, eyes scanning the freshly laid tables. "It was great to see you with friends on Friday night. Your smile! Light up the room! You do that more from now on, okay?" She patted Jillian's shoulder, turning as the golden bell jingled, announcing another arrival. Harry Jones, the butcher. Jillian smiled, nodding to him as she guzzled more water.

How can it be this hot this early in the morning? she cursed the Weather Gods.

Her aunt rushed off to greet Mr Jones, the 'Sausage King,' whose business prided itself on personally delivering fresh meat throughout town. He was a great friend to Duyin and Bao, as well as necessary to their business.

Friends...

"I promise to make more of an effort with my friends, both new and old," Jillian told her aunt's back, placing the note on the table and sliding her phone from the spandex pocket on her thigh.

Opening an old text chain, she winced at the date of the last communication.

Had it really been that long?

> Hey Breanna, long time no see. How are you these days?

Her fingers halted for a moment, then continued:

> I've been having a tough time since mum's passing. I'm not sure if you know or not …

Jillian deleted the sentence.

> I'm lonely and kind of utterly disappointed at how life has turned out thus far …

She erased that option, too.

She needed to write something simple.

Something she was ready to say.

> I miss you. I hope you're still in town and that we can catch up soon.

Jesus, how did she not know if one of her best friends still lived in Moonshine? For all Jillian knew, Breanna could have moved away ages ago!

Some friend you are, she berated herself, amending her message again.

> I miss you. I hope we can catch up soon x

Bre wasn't the only person she'd been neglecting recently.

Opening a new message, Jillian sent her sister a quick text.

> I'm sorry we haven't spoken since the funeral. I want to change that. I miss you. I'd love it if we could make time for a chat xo

She sent a similar message to her stepfather, Wayne, who would no doubt call her later and ask how to access the 'reply' feature on his phone. Inhaling deeply, pride rushed through her. Steps. She was taking baby steps. This was good.

Carefully tucking the red note back into the book, Jillian felt lighter than she had in months. Stepping out onto the main street, she inhaled deeply, the familiar smells of bread, coffee, and the headier farmyard smell of hay reaching deep into her soul, tugging the darkness from crevices they'd long inhabited.

Today will be a great day, she told herself, checking her watch.

She had an hour until her shift at Bloomin' Brilliant. Just enough time for some fresh brewed jet fuel.

As usual, Friday's Café was bursting with the caffeinated energy of happy patrons. The large Kiwi owner hustled behind his industrial coffee machine, grinding beans, filling the basket, extracting the perfect shot with a gorgeous golden layer of crema, and discarding the cookie.

The tiny, contented sucking sound of the swirling, frothing milk was bliss. There was nothing worse than an amateur sliding the jug up and down in some semi-sexual pantomime, while the milk squealed, and the steam wand forced huge bubbles into the mix.

"Finish that one already?" Friday's topknot wobbled in the direction of the book clasped in Jillian's hand. "There are plenty more MERI reads for you to swap it with."

She brought the book to her chest protectively. "Oh, no. I'm not done with it yet."

Friday's eyebrow raised, but he said no more, sliding her usual extra-large order across the counter. Their interactions were often limited to the minute or so it took him to create her liquid-reason-to-live.

"Have a great day," he said, smiling, already onto the next order.

"I will," she promised, eyes sliding to *Meet Me in Moonshine*. "I know I will."

It was a ridiculous decision, but Jillian waited until she got to work, wanting a safe space to read her Mystery Man's latest missive while sipping her coffee.

He made me wait a whole day, so a few minutes of reciprocal torture is in order, she told herself, snuggling into the stool beside a display of native banksias.

Dear J,
I am so sorry this note didn't make it into your hands earlier. The weekend was unexpectedly social.

He'd tried to erase the word 'social' but black pen was difficult to remove. Why was he trying to hide the fact his 'lonely' status was dwindling? That he had acted socially and enjoyed the company of people? Whatever his hesitation at the word, the mysterious D had obviously given up and continued.

My apologies for being ... disconnected. I hope you didn't think I'd abandoned you, or our quest to find out more about our town, and each other. I am loving our adventures, J. Truly. As a reward for your patience, I'll give you a hot tip. Dear Jesus, my hands are shaking as I'm writing this. See how

nervous you make me?

She inhaled deeply, reading on.

This Wednesday, I'll be at the greasy pig event at the Old Brumby Property, on Wattle Tree Road. I'm not sure if you've ever been before (I certainly haven't), but I've been convinced to attend. The thought of you being there too will make it much more tolerable.

Jillian had to turn the paper over to continue reading. Her cheeks were aching from the grin that had grown across her face.

Keep Meet Me in Moonshine *close by you over the next few days, lovely lady. I made you wait, so now it's my turn. 24 hours of torture.*

When you get to the Old Brumby Property, slip the book into old man Brumby's letterbox. The place is only available for event hire these days, so no one will be checking the letterbox regularly enough to intercept our notes.

Just so I know you stuck out the whole event, I'll reply during the day, and you can take Me home that night. Meet 'me' in Moonshine that is, not actually me me. Sorry, I'm strangely nervous right now. Promise you'll go?
With affection,
D-

Jillian squealed so loudly Iris came running, brandishing a

long-stalked sunflower, raised like a baton to fend off an attacker.

"Jillian, honey, what's wrong?" Iris dropped to her haunches, draping the bright sunflower across her lap.

"Nothing, I'm fine."

"Then why are you crying?"

"I'm not. Really, I'm fine." Her beaming smile must have convinced her boss to back off.

"Jillian, you're wearing spandex and joggers. Your unofficial life uniform is a floral dress. Are you sure there's nothing going on?"

"Oh, I'm sorry." Jillian looked down, flummoxed. "I can go home and change ..."

"That is not the point." Iris' gaze pierced her in a motherly, don't-bullshit-me kind of way, before she sighed. "You'd look great wrapped in a potato sack, Jillian. But if you say you're okay, I believe you. Now, if you're ready to work, there are customers ..."

"Sure thing, Boss!" Jillian chirped, "but, um, would you mind if I took Wednesday off? I know I was supposed to work, but–"

"Jillian, it's the lead up to Valentines! I need all hands on deck!"

"I know. You're right. I'm sorry." Shame and guilt pushed their way into her heart.

"Is this to do with that book? And the squealing?"

Her cheeks blushing the exact red of the banksias, Jillian nodded.

"Well –" Iris' voice softened, "I think one day can't hurt. But I will need you Thursday and Friday, okay?"

"Thank you, thank you!" Jillian wrapped a giggling Iris in a hug before sliding the book into her locker and skipping towards the shopfront.

Three orders and two arrangements later, Jillian's phone buzzed in the slinky pocket of her activewear. It was from Breanna Henderson:

> OMG Hi Jillian! I would LOVE to reconnect and catch up! How's tomorrow? The Pope? 11am?

It took Jillian less than a heartbeat to reply:

> Bloomin' brilliant! See you then x

Tuesday

THE POPE

As usual, THE POPE was full. Despite the early hour, the tavern had a reputation for always being open for business. Probably because the publican, Billy Carmichael, lived on site in one of the rooms above the bar.

The Pope was one of Moonshine's biggest claims to fame. The town's oldest tavern, it had established its liquor licence before the founding settlers had formally named the growing colonial township. Or so the local legends told.

Liquor was the religion of the bush, the tongue-in-cheek settlers aptly giving the pub a name with weight and honour.

The big, square building was a two-storey gem, built on one large city block. Constructed of old colonial sandstone,

The Pope boasted inviting antique heavy wood doors and open Victorian-style verandas added long ago to pack in more patrons. It had a cobbled courtyard that held memories of horses and carts, and an old carriage house that had been converted into a top-notch whiskey bar Billy hired out for events. Seating beneath two huge, shady English oak trees drew patrons into the courtyard, and back in time. Sandals clicking against the cobblestones, Jillian broke into a grin as she gripped the sun-warmed handle.

An old brass bell sung out her arrival. Halfway through pouring a beer one-handed, Billy looked up.

"Jillian Maitland!" his voice boomed. Slamming the schooner glass onto the counter, Billy rounded the bar to give her a one-armed squeeze. "Good to see you!" His rumbling voice rolled like thunder down a mountainside, reverberating through her chest.

"And you, Billy! Gosh, look at you! You're more muscle and tattoos than man these days!"

He laughed, flexing huge biceps, but only one forearm. Nearly every inch of his visible skin was covered in elaborate ink, the tattoos stretching out of his shirt, across his chest and almost into his beard as well. His light blue eyes winked at her and ... oh Jesus, he had dark hair too!

Are any males in this town red haired or green eyed or even bloody blond?

As though answering her prayers, another Moonshine High School survivor staggered past, burping.

Samuel Harthrup's floppy blond hair, bloodshot brown eyes and stained clothing told Jillian a sadder story than she wanted to know about him right now. And even though she'd just wished to see a man who couldn't possibly be a contender for her Mystery Man, Sam's appearance didn't provide the relief she'd expected. Yet somehow, it was comforting to know she wasn't the only one swimming in a sea of personal troubles.

"Go home, Sam," Billy growled. "Edith's come to get you."

"Shit, you called my gran?" Sam burp talked.

Gross.

Billy pointed out the door before placing his hand onto his hip in lieu of crossing his arms.

"Didn't leave me much choice, did you? The doc's busy, or else I would've harassed him a bit more."

"What use is a doctor for a best friend if you go running to my grandmother instead?" Sam slurred, tripping over his own feet as he wove a path to the door.

Snorting in farewell, or thanks (Jillian wasn't sure which), Sam stumbled into the street and towards a small white car where his grey-haired gran shot dagger-filled looks at him from the driver's seat.

Billy turned, shaking his head.

"I'm cutting him off. Nobody wants him to turn out like his parents."

Unconsciously, he rubbed at his white shirt, folded, and pinned crisply at the elbow, mumbling about 'accidents waiting to happen'.

In true small-town style, Jillian had known both Sam and Billy her entire life. Both were infamous, in a tragic way. The exact circumstances of Sam's story, she hated to remember.

His parents … Fresh waves of cold sorrow shot down her spine. Sam's story was less his than theirs. Their negligent actions had stunned all the adults in the town initially but ended in sighing and head shaking and familiar whispered conversations of how they'd 'expected it' all along.

Their actions had shaken the whole town, affecting Jillian's family personally, making Sam's schoolyard bullies back off in pity, and culminating in his living with his grandmother. From the look of him today, life hadn't improved much for Sam in the years since.

As they watched Sam slump into the seat and be driven away, Jillian considered the two men.

It intrigued her how a traumatic childhood event could affect two people in two different ways. Sam was drunk. Billy, stone cold sober. Kind of like how Jillian stayed in Moonshine, while her stepsister had fled to Sydney. Even those with the closest of tales wrote their own, unique stories.

Billy's history was just as infamous as Sam's. The difference was, everyone in town knew Billy's story, and he was its star. Sam kept his scars hidden inside while Billy wore his boldly. But, unlike Sam, Billy didn't have a choice.

At five years old, young Billy Carmichael and his brothers had been playing at the abandoned train yard. Around thirty trains had lain dormant in the rusting graveyard for as long as anyone could remember.

Jillian recalled a city-sider applying to develop the trainyard into a restaurant precinct, with a different string of carriages boasting different cuisine. For whatever reason, the project had never gone ahead, so the trains had remained parked, rusting, abandoned, in a large section of land running between the current train tracks and the Wollundry River.

For Billy, the yard had proved dangerous. Hide and seek had turned into life or death.

The old trains had been rusting in position since Federation, when the states had ditched separate lines to form one coherent national gauge.

Nobody quite knew how it happened, but that day, a train had moved. Billy's arm had been crushed. While his brothers had run into town, begging for help, young Billy Carmichael had lain unconscious for hours. This was long before kids had mobile phones. Before help was a swipe or button-push away.

Billy's arm had required amputation, the limb so badly crushed by the weighty train that there was no way to save it. Jillian shivered. She remembered reading the newspaper clipping about the tragedy, as if it were yesterday.

Funny how memory works.

The things you remember, like crying into your mother's shoulder, her damp blouse pressing against your cheek. And the things you forget, like the soothing words your mother gently whispered to make the world feel better again.

Billy had been flown via Care Flight to one of Sydney's top children's hospitals. Now here he was, alive and thriving in his thirties. He was easily the biggest, broadest man Jillian had ever seen. She watched him swipe his hand over his bearded chin.

"You drinking soft stuff or the hard stuff?"

"I don't have anywhere else to be ..."

She meant it to be a cute dismissal. *Sure, I can day-drink, I'm that cool.* But really, what she heard was the lame joke of someone with no real life to get back to.

"Been a bit worried about you, Jill," he rumbled, motioning for her to take a seat while he poured her favourite bar beverage – espresso martini.

Jillian couldn't help but smile.

"How do you always remember everyone's drink orders?" she marvelled.

"Steel trap," Billy tapped his temple. "Plus, I was there when you had your first coffee, remember? I'd only ever read about love at first sight, until that day. Seeing it for myself made me a believer." His Carmichael-blue eyes twinkled.

Every one of their clan were blessed with those piercing baby blues, so light they seemed almost angelic. *And totally at odds with his bad-boy, tattooed, hairy-biker-like exterior,* she mused, smiling at Billy.

"But don't go changing the subject." His eyes locked onto hers, and held warning.

Jillian sighed. Billy wasn't just physically massive, he was as immovable as a mountain. Once he latched onto something, it didn't have a chance of escape until he had finished with it.

This quality had made him a great friend in the past. He'd been the first to notice and try to fix her first period of social isolation.

When her father had left, it had been Billy who'd told Breanna something was wrong, insisting Jillian needed their help. He'd enlisted Adam and Breanna to organise a 'girls' night', during which Breanna pampered Jillian with love and nail polish and girly movies.

The boys had sworn it 'wasn't their thing', eventually climbing the lattice of the house she still lived in to sneak in the window at midnight with popcorn, singing along with John Travolta in *Grease*. How Billy managed it with only one arm, she'd never know.

Her mother had simply giggled at their off-key antics through the closed door, despite The Rules clearly stating *Boys + Bedrooms = Hell No*.

Jillian had never loved her mum so much. And when their family grew, when Wayne and Clarissa had moved in, the sleepovers had only become more enjoyable. Almost overnight, a school friend became her sister, and that had made all the difference.

Jillian remembered so clearly the night Billy had shown their sleepover crew his stump, the nub of flesh at the elbow where his lower limb had been amputated. Billy's courage to share his own pain, in his own way, encouraged her to return to the world, too.

The words 'hot zombie' filtered into her head once more. *At least they'd brought popcorn.* Jillian smiled fondly at the memory. *All Oscar brings is his bed-hogging attitude.*

"So," Billy's gruff voice pressed on as he single handedly wiped the bar and loaded glassware into the dishwasher. "How have you been? Haven't seen you since the funeral ..." He paused, as though unsure if he should go on. "And we missed you at Christmas."

Christmas was to the Carmichaels as honey was to the bees. Every year they had a massive shindig on their property, a large farm that supplied many families with the perfect Christmas tree and ample cheer. Two months ago, she hadn't been able to face the world. Despite their long-held tradition, she hadn't attended the Carmichael's Christmas.

"I'm sorry," she told the wooden bar, the condensation from her glass running over her fingertips. "And honestly? I'm not great." *It feels so good to admit it.*

Unconsciously one hand searched the physical comfort of the book in her bag. "But I'm trying to reconnect with the world, you know?"

"I do know." His piercing, soulful eyes met hers. "I know a bit about loss and disconnect."

Billy wasn't a big talker. Years of experience had proven him to be a grunt-and-nod kind of guy who could communicate more with a look than words. For him to be talking so openly now, spoke volumes about their friendship and reconnection. *I need this. I need you and Bre and ...*

An intense air settled for a few long moments, before he nodded, almost growling. "Heard you saw Adam the other night."

"I did." Jillian smiled as hazy memories from last Friday night flicked through her mind. "Do you see him often?"

"Too bloody often," Billy grumbled, his deep voice shaking through the last of her reverie. "Women fawn all over him, practically strip him off to touch him all over. If I have to tell him to put his shirt on one more time ..." The publican shook his head.

Most people would run after a first-and-only warning from any of the Carmichael brothers. But Adam knew better than to believe Billy's tough exterior. That, and Adam's impressive ego, would not result in any shirt-on action. And Billy knew it.

"He's got nothing on you, Muscle Man." Jillian squeezed his bicep like she had all those years ago, when he'd started going to the gym and filling out.

Conversations of the past haunted her.

"You have nothing to prove, Billy," she'd told the teenaged version of this man, watching him struggle with a weight.

"Not to them," he'd grunted, curling and flexing his bicep, breathing through the set. "Just to myself."

Just to myself...

Billy said something, snapping the present back into place.

"Sorry, what?"

"I said thanks, Daisy." Billy smirked now, his large tattooed hand patting hers, humour sparking in his light eyes.

"Oh my God, will *anyone* ever forget those damn denim shorts?"

"Not in this lifetime." He flashed straight white teeth behind his bearded jaw. "We all have our claim to fame, Daisy Duke. Be glad yours only involves fashion." Nodding in farewell, he travelled up the bar to welcome new patrons.

"Jill!" A familiar voice nearly made her fall off the bar stool. "Oh, Jill! It is you!" Breanna rushed into Jillian's already open arms. They hugged for a long, long time, Jillian leaning down awkwardly from her bar stool. Eventually, Breanna pulled back, sniffling, her eyes misty. "Holy shit I've missed you, Jill."

"Looks like I've missed a fair bit of you, too!" Jillian grinned at Breanna's big, round belly. "May I?"

"Thank Christ you asked. So many people don't and it's like, why are you putting hands onto me, you random? But you're not some random weirdo in the tampon aisle. Of course, you can! Feel my baby bump, Jill! Go on! I reckon the little shit's going to claw its way out if I keep eating your aunt's bird's nest soup. But, you know, cravings."

Jillian ran her hands around Breanna's bubbling, taut belly, feeling the aforementioned 'little shit' squirming beneath her friend's skin.

"Cool. Strange," Jillian marvelled, feeling the baby roll and kick.

"You should feel it from the inside. So fricking weird, Jill. Let me grab a water from Billy and we can chat somewhere comfier."

Billy promised to bring a carafe to the table immediately. "Don't break my furniture, heifer," he teased.

"If it can hold your bulky ass, bed-breaker, then it'll certainly hold me," Breanna retorted, eyebrow raised.

Billy's thunderous laughter shook the walls. *Only Bre could ever make him laugh like that,* Jillian mused, caught up in his mirth. She grabbed her espresso martini, certain the glass might smash if she didn't protect it from the soundwaves that came with Billy's rare yet powerfully explosive laughs.

"Bed-breaker?" Jillian grinned up at Bre's round belly.

"Long story from years ago, back before ..." Bre grunted out a satisfied noise as she sat down heavily on the edge of a Chesterfield sofa, leaning forward so her belly settled between wide-spread knees. "And all four of our brothers were involved, so nothing suss."

Billy and Bre had been thick as thieves for most of their lives, neighbours and literally partners in crime at one stage. Billy was a closed book, but Bre ... she was much more forthcoming.

"Actually, that sounds *way* suss, Bre." Jillian giggled into her espresso martini, eyeing her friend. "Forgive me for saying this," she added, "but you're huge!"

"Urgh, I know. Disgustingly glorious, isn't it? I waited my whole life for big breasts and womanly curves – and now I feel like a hippo and look like a bag of marbles!" Jillian loosed a laugh as Breanna moaned with pleasure, leaning back to put her feet up on the coffee table.

Billy cleared his throat, a sound like grinding rocks. "Feet? Table. Off."

Breanna didn't even open her eyes to respond. "Find me an ottoman and I will. Until then, these swollen ankles need elevation. And I'd love water. Plenty of ice. The more ice, the merrier!" She waved him off with a flick of her fingers.

Grumbling, Billy disappeared again.

There was no arguing with Breanna Henderson. Having grown up with five boys (one being her biological brother and the four Carmichael clansmen themselves) Bre had learned long ago how to get her way when it came to TWP (or, *Those With Penises*, as they'd called them in school).

"I'm so glad you texted." Breanna fixed her with a look, causing Jillian to inhale her martini. Patiently, she waited for Jillian to stop spluttering and coughing. "I knew you would, you know. You're a boomerang, baby, you'll always come back. Just in your own time. I wish I'd made an effort to reconnect sooner, though, to tell you all about this." Bre's palm swept over her gigantic belly and the rolling baby who looked like it was trying to escape, like some alien in a horror film, just below the surface.

"I'm here now," Jillian said, reaching out to hold her oldest friend's hand. "And you can tell me anything." Her vision became blurred and watery.

"I want to hear about you first." Breanna's eyes welled in empathy with her friend. "I heard about your mum ... Jill, I'm so sorry. You should have said something!"

"I ... I couldn't. I didn't know how. I just kind of imploded, you know? And I assumed Billy would have mentioned it ..." Jillian sniffed, sipping her drink and steadying her nerves. "We'd been waiting for it, honestly. She was ready. I don't think I ever would have been ready, but now ..." She sighed, battling back tears. "I think I'm starting to move forward again." She laughed wryly. "But I've been unintentionally neglecting my stepfather and –"

"Your sister?"

"Yeah. Her too. I just ... I don't know what to say to them,

I suppose. So, I stopped talking." Jillian laughed dryly again. "Adam called me a hot zombie. That's pretty much how I feel most days, death warmed up. But it's getting easier."

She didn't want to discuss *Meet Me in Moonshine*, or her lonely Mystery Man and his adventurous plan for them both to reengage in the world. For now, it was just nice to sit comfortably with an old friend and sip on her icy, coffee-flavoured martini.

"You've seen Adam?" Bre's eyes lit up. "He's really grown into his ..." Jillian fixed her with a look and Breanna coughed lightly, rolling her eyes, "– ego. I was going to say *ego!*" The women burst into giggles, Bre's belly shaking with the effort. "But seriously, Jill, I never understood why you were immune to Adam's sexy powers. Is it because he treats you like a little sister? Especially after everything that happened with your sis–" She paused. "But let's not go down that rabbit hole. I'm glad to hear *you're* doing okay ... *ish*."

Breanna squeezed Jillian's hand, dropping it to sigh in bliss as Billy swung her still-elevated feet onto a small, circular ottoman.

"You're a God, Billy Carmichael, I swear it."

"Yeah, well, don't swear too loudly. You know I don't like bawdy women."

"Who even says *bawdy*?"

"People," he huffed, "who read." Billy's bulk turned away, returning what seemed like seconds later with a tall glass of iced water for Breanna.

The man's a human tornado, Jillian thought, watching him work, awestruck.

"I think he gets cuter every time I see him." Breanna smirked. "And more tattooed."

Jillian snorted, rolling her eyes. "I don't think *cute* is the word for Billy Carmichael ..."

"How about handy?"

"Bre! You can't say that!"

"I don't mean it like *that*!" Bre insisted, leaning closer over her beach-ball belly. "Did you know, he got sucked into Adam's truth-or-dare shenanigans one time and slipped his fingers straight down my shorts and –"

Jillian exploded into shrieks of laughter, cheeks red and eyes wide as she *shushed* her friend. Breanna had no shame.

Billy shot them a look and Jillian smothered her open mouth.

"He didn't!" she whispered, still snorting through her fingers and shooting sidelong looks at the one-armed publican.

"Well, I wasn't pregnant at the time!"

"Would it have made a difference?"

Breanna pretended to consider this, a wicked grin playing at her lips.

"You haven't changed, Bre."

"Thank God for that, hey?" Breanna considered Jillian. "You have, though, Jill. Your hair's longer and you have more freckles. Means you're getting out, which is awesome." She rested both hands on her belly, maternally. "It's more than that, though. You've got a bit of a glow happening over there. Like, you're finally ready to be the leading lady in your own story, you know? You look one step away from the spotlight. It's nice." Breanna moaned, shifting in her chair. "Bub needs me to move. And I need to pee. Help me to my car?"

"You're going to pee in your car?"

"No, silly! I still can't use public restrooms. The *germs*!" Bre shivered, waddling and leaning heavily on Jillian's arm.

"Don't let Billy hear you say that," Jillian giggled. "You know he'd be down on hand and knees scrubbing instantly. The man's a whirlwind."

"And he'd do anything for us." Bre added, making tired, breathless noises as they shuffled outside The Pope.

Balking, Jillian spluttered. "How long were we in there?"

Dusk had fallen and a flock of noisy galahs had settled into the trees, squawking as though their lives depended on it. Sliding her phone from her bag, she stared as the screen lit up, proudly telling her it was dinner time. *Well, that explains the sudden explosion of patrons at the pub.* The after-work crowd had settled in hours ago.

Leaning in, Breanna pulled *Meet Me in Moonshine* from Jillian's bag.

"What's this?" She turned Jillian's treasure in her hands. "I know this book."

Jillian's heart skipped a beat. "You do?"

"Yeah. I met the author." Breanna winced. "And I *really* need to pee."

"Oh ... My ... God."

"It's fine. My pelvic floor is like a Pandora's box. Locked down, baby."

Jillian didn't have the heart to explain Greek mythology right now. "Not that, Breanna. The author!"

"Oh. You don't need to fangirl about it. He's a local guy. I met him at a Moonshine Historical Society meet-and-greet, right here at The Pope, but I know where he lives. Not because I'm some stalker," she chuckled unconvincingly, "but because he was so into showing me photos of the place. He's just renovated it for the Heritage Council."

He'd been right here? At The Pope? When?

Gulping, Jillian fought for words, asking the foremost question in her mind. "What does he look like?"

Bre obviously didn't hear her strangled tone. Grinning, she barrelled into an explanation that lit Jillian's imagination like a Christmas tree.

"Oh, Jill, he's super handsome! And very smart. Tall, dark, and these *delicious* blue eyes. He's got legs for days, they're so long. But, I mean, I'm five-foot-nothing, so I'm not the best judge ..." Bre gripped Jillian's forearm, grabbing her attention. Jillian met her friend's eyes. "Seriously, Jill, his thighs, oh my lord, Jillian, they are *glorious*. What I wouldn't give to see that man in his board shorts ..." Breanna moaned in pleasure at the thought, rubbing her hands over her stomach.

Jillian's mouth had gone completely dry, her brain slotting each puzzle piece into place.

"But ignore me. I'm just super horny from all the hormones racing around." Breanna leaned in to hug Jillian, kissing her cheek in farewell. "Ew, Jill, you're all hot and sweaty! You should go shower. And please don't leave it so long until our next catch up." She chuckled, sliding awkwardly behind the wheel of her car.

"I won't," Jillian promised, trying desperately to avoid asking for more details about her mystery note writer.

I might see him tomorrow. At the pig thing.

Would she even recognise this man? Her perfect stranger?

A thought hit her suddenly, like lightning to her brain.

Yanking open the heavy wooden door, Jillian called back into The Pope.

"Hey Billy, what the heck is this greasy pig event?"

Wednesday

THE OLD BRUMBY HOMESTEAD

JILLIAN HADN'T SLEPT SO badly since she had accidentally (on purpose) downed six double shot cappuccinos in one day. All night, lines from D's latest note floated through her mind, settling in warm patches in her chest.

I am loving our adventures, J. Truly ...

See how nervous you make me? ...

The thought of you being there too will make it much more tolerable ... lovely lady.

Promise you'll go? ...

With affection ...

Her reply was burning a hole through her hand as she read it one more time, agonising over every word.

My Dear D,

Was that too forward? Too affectionate? Was the 'my' too possessive?

I've never been to this greasy pig thing, so today will be ... interesting. I don't know if I'll know anybody there, so I'll be the loner who sticks out like a sore thumb.

I did ask my friend to come, but she's extremely pregnant ...

Jillian scrubbed the last two words out.

Jesus, I can't write that!

She could have kicked herself. Jillian couldn't share their possible connection to Breanna. Not now. Sure, there were probably many pregnant women in town right now, but she couldn't give unnecessary clues too soon. If D was teaching her anything with this scavenger hunt, it was that romance required a little mystery.

I did ask my friend to come, but she's unavailable.

Jillian marvelled at how edited their notes were becoming, with both parties reconsidering word choices, implications, and tone before sliding their letter into the book.

Anyway, see you today (even if I don't recognise you). I look forward to reading your highlight from today when I collect **Meet Me in Moonshine,** *after the event.*

Taking a deep breath, she pushed on.

I was wondering, if it wouldn't be too forward, if we should meet? In real life, I mean? It wouldn't have to be a date or anything. Nothing too scary or official or whatever. Ha, now I'm the nervous one. Isn't this ridiculous?
Let me know your thoughts.
Yours,
J- x

The book was inside the old letterbox now, and she wasn't brave enough to put her hand into the spider-infested converted wine barrel to drag it back out and rip that last section off.

Whoever the mysterious Mister D was, he didn't suffer arachnophobia, or was just super brave, or had no idea the letterbox was a spider infested hell hole.

She had never been to the Old Brumby Property on Wattle Tree Road before, but it was as beautiful as any romanticised image of bush life Banjo Paterson might have described.

The property was no longer a working farm, but a series of buildings, courtyards, gardens, and open fields where tourists could enjoy a quiet country break. The main house was a Federation-style homestead, all angles and built to last.

At the entrance to the property, sitting between tall grey eucalypts, were three cottages neatly labelled 'Brumby's Carriage House', 'Servant's Quarters' and 'The Gardner's Cottage'. Each had been meticulously restored and, like the gardens, gleamed for this event.

A cloud of dust kicked up as she rolled her Swift into a shaded park between two trees.

"Bye, air-con," she sighed as her boots crunched to the ground. Tugging her shorts down, she followed the crowd.

"Been here before, love?" A white-bearded farmer greeted her at the gated entrance, taking the minimal entry fee in exchange for a raffle prize ticket.

"Is it that obvious?" Jillian looked down at her outfit. The Daisy Dukes had come out of retirement, and half her arse was hanging out of the shorts.

"You need a hat, love." The old man winked, taking the wide-brimmed Akubra off his own head and plonking it onto hers. "Just give it back after the show's over, alright? Now go on, get inside." He pushed her gently through the gate, already welcoming the long line of people behind her.

"HELLO AND WELCOME TO THE SEVENTY-EIGHTH ANNUAL VALENTINE'S GREASY PIG CHASE DAY!" echoed a man's voice from a loudspeaker.

119

"PROCEEDINGS WILL COMMENCE SHORTLY, SO STRETCH THOSE LEGS AND GULP THEM BEERS. THIS YEAR'S PIGGY'S A LIVE ONE!"

How can I have lived here all my life and not know about this event? she wondered, bending, as instructed, to loosen her calf muscles.

A heavy hand slapped her arse. "Hello there," a man's voice drawled.

Stiffly, Jillian straightened, turning on her heel to confront the chauvinist. As she spun, her foot caught one of the many protruding roots from the ancient eucalypts that stretched above. In a spectacular flurry, she stumbled, falling to the dirt.

The pig (hopefully not the kind this event had been named for) snorted, sculling his drink as he leered over her.

"Want a hand?" He licked his lips as the words came out, his eyes sliding from her head to her toes then back up to linger on her chest.

Disgust slid like sweat over her skin. "Not from you!" she spat.

A familiar form forced its way between her and the pig who had touched her.

"Back off, mate," his voice said, her protector's chest seeming to grow wider with every millisecond of tension between the two men.

A wall of rippling, taut muscle towered over her aggressor now. Jillian shrunk into the dirt. After a few tense moments, the jerk retreated, and her saviour turned.

"Adam!" Relief drew her shoulders down from her ears. How did Adam appear out of thick, hot air when she was in trouble?

"Dais, you okay?"

Better now.

Her friend easily bore her weight as she pulled herself up. Adam patted dirt from her gently, assessing for damage.

"Glad to see these babies out of retirement," he chuckled, looping a finger through one pocket of her denim shorts. "You're lookin' real cute there, Daisy Duke."

You're not so bad yourself, mister ... He was owning a rockstar-cowboy kind of look today, like a sexy country singer or rodeo star who had just stepped from some high-end magazine shoot.

Adam saw her appraising him, grinning a lopsided acknowledgement, before pulling his Akubra low over his eyes.

Yeah, you know *you look good, Adam James.* He played coy, but she wouldn't fall for it. *I won't compliment you just to stroke your ego, and you know it!*

"All the boys got dressed up," he confessed, tugging at his checked shirt, only highlighting the trim cut of his body beneath.

"Looks like you fit in well." Jillian nodded to the crowd, a sea of plaid, denim, and wide-brim hats. "Thanks for your help back there. I'm actually really glad to find someone I know." *Because I am waaaay outside my comfort zone, here, buddy.* Now it was her turn to adjust her hat awkwardly.

"Yeah, us fellas come out to Brumby's most years to snag a decent Valentine's dinner. We brought a few ring-ins this year, so you'll be in good company. And old Les said they took nearly three hundred dollars at the gate, so the winner gets that too."

"What? Are you even speaking English right now?"

Adam grinned, reminding her his school experiences could more accurately be likened to tuition by Casanova than Shakespeare. Rolling her eyes, Jillian could only shake her head.

"LADIES AND GENTLEMEN, GET READY AT THE START LINE!" the announcer's voice declared, echoing off the buildings and into the open field.

Like sheep, they followed the crowd towards the courtyard to one side of the main house.

"Whatever, Adam. But always remember, I know your secret."

He laughed. "And that is?"

"You're so much more than a pretty man-whore. You're also a tragic *Grease* fan who owns every Olivia Newton John –"

"SSSSHHHH!!!!" Adam's hand pressed down on Jillian's mouth, eyes pleading as they stopped amidst the crowd.

"No more, please, Daisy."

"Okay. I'll zip it. But you have to tell me exactly what this event is because, quite frankly, I'm at a loss."

He gave her a quizzical look. "You don't know what today's about?"

"GET READY."

"Well, Dais, you'll soon find out!"

"GET SET!"

Somewhere in the distance, a pig squealed.

"GO!"

The crowd moved like rainbow sprinkles tipped into a bowl, all taking their own directions and crashing into others.

Adam took off, tickling a young lady as he passed. She screamed, kicking up her feet and swatting flirtatiously at him.

Like the rest of the crowd, Jillian erupted into squeals and laughter as she jumped and dodged men, women and children who fell over each other.

A pig – *a real-life pig!* – weaved between and among their legs. It was a shiny brown colour, glistening.

"They greased it up real good this year," someone complained, wiping espresso-coloured slime down the front of their pants.

"Oh, Jesus," Jillian said, sliding off to one side and around the corner of a building.

The crowd spread out.

Some herded the pig in a coordinated attempt. Others chased after it, lunging desperately, only to have it slip through their hands. Most of the crowd ran squealing from fun as the animal chased them, switching direction every few steps.

"REMEMBER FOLKS, THE FUN PART IS PLAYING THE GAME," the announcer said, chuckling. Jillian looked to the clouds. Her mother used to say that all the time.

Is this a sign, Mum? Really? A slippery pig chase?

"You better get in there, love," the whiskered Akubra-gifting man encouraged. Les, Adam had called him. "Pig will keep on running or go to ground, hiding. If it makes it past the fence there, well, let's just say the property's bigger than you'd think."

"What happens if it isn't caught?"

"Well," Les scratched his chin, pondering. "The event is done when the pig's caught, and some of the blokes are ready for an evening shoot if they have to, so try and catch the little fella in the light if you can. Plus, three hundred bucks." He fanned a wad of notes before his face. "Nice little treat for yourself, or your loved one, this Valentine's Day."

Ah yes, *The Day*.

"If anything," she muttered, stomping off, away from the crowd, "I could buy myself a really nice birthday present." Eyes to the ground, Jillian began her search for the prized greasy pig.

An hour later, she was feeling stupid.

Ridiculous and stupid.

She had wandered too far in God knew which direction. The Brumby Homestead was a dot she could barely see down the hill through the trees. Even smaller black dots moved around the property, the crowd dwindling to congregate at what looked like a makeshift bar on the shady porch of the house. The trail she was currently following wound its way through increasingly bushy land.

Jillian didn't have much porcine experience, but she assumed the little oinker wouldn't have run this far afield. Kicking the dirt, she felt frustration settle with the dust.

She had been too worried about her stupid, butt-smacking, attention-grabbing shorts, and a *pig* of all things, to even consider her primary goal – to play 'spot the Mystery Man' in the crowd.

Was the Moonshine-loving, mysterious Mister D here? Had he retrieved *Meet Me in Moonshine* from the arachnid-infested box? Or was this all just a stupid, *stupid* idea and a total waste of time?

Her phone buzzed. Iris Bloom's picture smiled up at her from the screen.

Oh, Jesus. Bloody hell.

"Hello?" she replied.

There was a rustling nearby.

"Jillian? Honey, are you okay? I thought you were coming in today?" Worry was thick in her boss' voice. "Or have I forgotten something? You know that is likely."

"Iris, I am so sorry, I –"

A pink and brown blur zipped past her feet. The faintest outline of a curly tail spurred her to action.

"I've gotta go!"

Ending the call, Jillian took off after the animal. It darted into a clearing, heading for the shady underbelly of an old shearers' shed.

Damn!

It disappeared beneath the splinter-infested building.

"Here, piggy piggy piggy," she sung, bending to peek under the oily-smelling floor. The shadows moved. Tiny grunting breaths gave her hope this would all be over soon. "Pig, I promise I won't eat you. I just want the prize money so I can treat myself to some bubble bath and new knickers for my birthday. Maybe a vibrator, the way this year's going. Is that too much to ask?"

A deep, warm chuckle overlaid the pig's panting. "I think maybe you should say please."

Jillian threw herself vertical, smashing the back of her head against something hard.

"OW!" the man cried. "My nose!"

Spinning on her heel, Jillian's eyes widened.

"Jesus, Coffee-Killer, what are you even doing here? Why are you sneaking up on people?"

The shape darted out from the shadows.

"Pig!"

Jillian threw herself to the ground, pinning the squealing, wriggling creature.

Despite its relatively small size, it was a powerful little thing. Its hooves scratched her arms and needle-like hairs stabbed her chest as she held it tightly, legs scratching along the ground as she scrambled for control.

Its head was now motor boating into her bosom. *Seriously? The most action I've had in … forever … is with Porky Pig?!* Her grip loosened.

"It's slipping!"

"Grab its legs!" he shouted, hands slipping on residual grease. Cursing, he ordered, "Close your eyes!"

"What? Why?" she asked, just as he threw a huge handful of dirt all over her. Spitting bark, tiny rocks and shock to the ground, Jillian almost let go of the squirming swine.

"Grab it! The dirt helps with grip."

"Grab what? I can't see thanks to you!"

The pig had nearly twisted from her grasp and there was no way to blink the dust from her eyes.

"The collar, woman. The collar!"

"It has a collar?" Blinking was futile, but she tried, tears streaming down her cheeks.

"Just trust me! Do it!"

"Aw, man, I haven't had enough coffee for this shit."

Jillian loosened her arms. The wiggling pig slid through her hands. Somehow, she found the strap.

Looping her fingers through, she felt the choking tug of the poor creature as her partner in crime jumped onto it like a bull rider, ready for the ring. For a tiny thing, the wriggling bacon put up a mighty fight.

The Coffee-Killer gripped the pig's body between his thighs, pinning it to the ground with his weight, looping a length of rope through its collar. Panting, he told her to let go of the wiggling pig.

"You sure?"

"It's leashed!" he insisted, sweat glistening on his brow. "Let go, Daisy!"

No need to tell me twice!

The prize tried to dart off again, this time securely fastened to Dimple's tight-gripped leash. Coughing, dripping in sweat, slick with grease and sticky with dirt, Jillian thought, *Fuck this. I'm done.*

"Let me tie this bugger to a tree to calm down," Dimples mumbled, footsteps crunching their way through bush. Jillian sucked in deep lungful of air, wiping at her face with dirty, greasy hands, and trying desperately to stay upbeat.

"Pig wrestling is surprisingly tough exercise," she coughed, wincing as more dirt dislodged from her brow and fell into her eyes. Dimples flashed Jillian a smile, earning his nickname, which she barely saw through her bush-dust crusted eyes.

"Oh, Christ, sorry about the dirt thing." His blurred form quickly unbuttoned its shirt and started gently wiping at her face. Loosening dirt and more tears, they both breathed hard from exertion. His breath, hot and ragged, beat at her temple. "Hold on," he said, striding to an old water bucket beside the shearing shed and dunking his shirt in. Wringing it slightly, he strode back.

"Let me fix this." The sweet scent of coffee lingered on his breath. He wiped her skin, which cooled in the wake of his makeshift face washer. Still panting, his unsteady breath matched hers.

Jillian's heartbeat slowed, her stomach growling.

"Hungry?" he said, onto her temple. He was so close. She could have counted each freckle splattered across the bridge of his nose, if she'd wanted. *One. Two ... Twenty-three.*

"Yes," she sighed, resisting the urge to lean into the cool

dampness of his touch. "For pork."

She snatched at the soaked shirt. This was a competition, and she needed to win. She hooked her finger through the fabric before dragging it where it needed to go.

He puffed out exhausted laughter. "Alright, alright. Don't go getting those denim knickers in a twist." His dimples deepened.

"They're *shorts*, not underwear." Jillian's smirk ruined her resolution.

"Could've fooled me, Daisy." His deepening smirk forced laughter from them both.

As their breathing slowed and the pig stopped squealing its complaints, Dimples held out his hand in offering. Slapping it away, she pushed off the dirty bush floor so fast it made her head spin.

Snatching up the Akubra, she pulled it down deftly onto her head before tripping over the pig's extended rope.

The animal squealed in surprise, mimicking Jillian's shriek. Dimples laughed, loud and strong, the ghosts of the farm echoing his humour.

"Careful there, Daisy," he said through his chuckles. "You put up a good fight, but it's a bit unfair now he's tied to a gumtree!"

The twin grooves in his cheeks were doing something funny to her insides, cutting through the seriousness of his remarks.

"I never thought I'd be able to say I wrestled a pig *and won*." She giggled, adrenaline thumping through her veins in a way coffee probably never would again. Dimples' blue eyes crinkled into warm lines as he joined her merriment.

What. Is. Your. Name? She longed to ask, trying desperately to remember if it has been uttered, as he re-buttoned his blue checked shirt. *Are you him? The man I'm trying to find? The one I keep hoping to meet in Moonshine?*

"We should get back and claim our prize money," he said, untying the pig from the tree.

"Excuse me? *Our* money?" They started the long walk back to the Brumby Homestead.

"Well, yeah. You. Me. Fifty, fifty." He shrugged.

"No way, bucko, the prize is mine, fair and square. I found the pig and I damn near squished it with that belly flop attack. All you did was tie a rope and shower me in dirt! Hardly equal share in three hundred bucks."

"Okay, how about we make a deal?"

Jillian narrowed her eyes. "What kind of deal?"

He stopped to face her, cheeks burnt from the day in the sun. She could smell his sweat-infused David Beckham cologne. He leaned in so close she could count his freckles. *Twenty-four freckles. Twenty-five* ... Bre's comment about her own freckles flitted through her mind.

So, you spend a fair amount of time outside, hey Dimples?

"How about we go on a date? You, me, Babe here." He inclined his head to their now much calmer pet pig. "We could eat the third wheel ..."

Jillian's mouth dropped open at his suggestion.

"Or go on a spree and spend our three hundred dollars together." He reset his eyes to the Homestead, continuing the walk. "Valentine's Day is coming up, you know."

"I know." She groaned.

"And from what I heard, before you attacked Porky here," he grinned, eyes fixed ahead, "your birthday plans were a bit lacking, too, in certain regards." He turned pointedly, raising an eyebrow and her temperature. Jillian wanted to shrivel up under a bush and die.

The vibrator.

Oh, Jesus, how absolutely mortifying. He *had* heard her comment to the damn pig.

"I'll bring the coffee, you bring the beer, and separately we'll sip and avoid sticky, stained clothing?" he jokingly offered. *Sticky, stained clothing? ...* Did he even know what he was implying?

Probably not. She watched the dawning realisation change the lines of his face. The Coffee-Killer started to backtrack.

"Oh, shit, I mean ... what I mean is ..."

Move over, Adam James, a new sexy-talking charmer is in town. Any man who could boil her kettle by talking coffee was definitely date material.

Dimples took a deep breath, his long strides slowing. "Would you like to go on a date?" His red cheeks darkened a shade.

Jillian opened her mouth to answer, but before a single syllable could form, a cheer rang out across the paddock. Sweaty, dirty, greasy people swarmed towards them.

Dimples pressed the rope into her hand and stood back, joining the crowd. Clapping, whistling, and cheering, they acted like she'd just won an Academy Award or Olympic Gold Medal rather than caught a slippery, greased-up pig.

Jillian was filthy, embarrassed, and most of all, she was proud of herself.

Her heart grew three sizes as the whiskery greeter slapped her on the back, pressing a wad of cash into her free hand.

"Well done," Les whispered, patting her sweaty, stained back.

"Let's hear it for Daisy!" Adam pushed his way to the front, clapping wildly and revving up the crowd.

"To Daisy!" The gathering cheered.

Dimples swiped off her hat to drop a small, hot kiss on her forehead before shoving a squealing, startled pig into her arms.

Thursday

BLOOMIN' BRILLIANT

Spiderman. Her Mystery Man must be some spider immune hero. *Not that Spiderman was immune ...* she pondered. *He was certainly spider-affected.*

"Maybe I need a new analogy."

And I really, really need to stop talking to animals and inanimate objects, little troublemakers! With the sex-toy comment lingering in the Most Embarrassing Moments of Jillian's Life highlight reel, she shook her head.

After many congratulations and babysitting arrangements made for her new pig, she had returned to the old Brumby letterbox late yesterday afternoon. Not a spider or clinging web was present. Whoever the note-writer was, he was thoughtful and clearly had no fear. Jillian added these facts to her growing list of 'pros'.

Meet Me in Moonshine had been tucked safely into its hiding place. A small bunch of wildflowers lay gently resting on top. Despite the absolute strangeness of the Greasy Pig Day, she was beyond exhilarated, cheeks aching all over again. Pressing the wildflowers to her chest, she had practically squealed into their vibrant heads.

As she drove back into town, her thoughts tumbled into worry. The one thorn in her day of roses was Iris Bloom. Guilt clawed at Jillian's insides for skipping her shift at the florist.

Valentine's Day for florists was *The Day*. It was Christmas for roses, but without all the tinsel. Valentine's Day was the one day a year when the world stopped and remembered to love nature, both botanical and human. *And I am leaving my boss, my friend, in the lurch as she prepares for this massive event.*

"It can't happen again," she had told Oscar after her third shower (one hadn't been enough to rid her of the grease, sweat and pervasive stink of pig shit that clung to her skin). Oscar hasn't cared for her complaining or her plans, but he did find Jillian's new scent curious. Perceiving her day had been out of the ordinary, he'd even relinquished his full reign of the bed last night, curling into her neck rather than into the centre of their co-sleeping space.

Sleepily, she drew the small wildflower bouquet from her bedside table, inhaling them gently, hoping to find a clue, perhaps the lingering scent, of her thoughtful note writer. Sliding *Meet Me in Moonshine* closer, Jillian flicked through the pages for a tell-tale red slip.

The note, caught between two images of the historic train station that made her instantly think of Billy, was quickly removed. Desperate to hear about his day, Jillian tried to read D's words, but residual dirt and exhaustion gave everything a hazy quality. Blinking and washing her face (again) didn't help to make the note any clearer.

Too tired to keep her eyes open any longer, Jillian clutched her letter and curled in the sheets, *her* sheets, slipping quickly into sleep.

At 5am, Thursday morning, 'Here Comes the Sun' by The Beatles filtered from her phone.

"Good kitty," she purred, rolling to switch off her alarm. "Sorry it's so early, but there's something I have to do."

An array of birds were already twittering, despite the dark of early morning. *The early bird catches the worm.* Who would have ever imagined her catching both worms and a pig in two days?

Stumbling into the kitchen, Jillian made an unsatisfying instant coffee before heading back upstairs to get ready for the day.

From the dry heat already in the air, it was going to be another stiflingly hot Australian summer day.

I really *need to get that cooler fixed* ... Jillian mentally added 'call an air conditioning technician' to her To Do list. Selecting a light cotton dress from her expansive floral collection, Jillian headed for the shower.

A little later she stuck her head round the bedroom door and said, "See you tonight?" The sleepy cat meowed and resumed his comfortable spot.

Jillian slid into her Swift and drove to Bloomin' Brilliant, hours before opening time.

At 7:30am, Iris slid her key into the door and stepped into the florist. Bloomin' Brilliant was spotlessly clean, counter tops gleaming, fresh bouquets prepared, and new, elaborate arrangements placed into the window displays beside foil balloons that read 'Be My Valentine'.

"Jillian ..." Iris spun in slow circles, eyes wide. "This is to die for! Did you do all this?"

"You know I did." She smiled at her boss. "And here's a fresh almond milk latte from Friday's Café. He wasn't finished prepping the breakfast burritos, but he said he'd have one delivered shortly."

"Oh, Jillian." Iris' eyes misted as the hot takeaway cup was placed into her hands, and her gaze swept over what looked like a new store. "This is just lovely. Thank you, honey."

"You deserve it." Jillian smiled, pleased with her work.

You deserve this, deserve better than me ...

"I let you down, and I'm sorry. You've *never* let me down, Iris. Never. Even when Mum ..." Her voice cracked, but Jillian forced her words through the lump in her throat. "Even when Mum got her diagnosis and was having treatment, you were there."

Iris wrapped Jillian in her long, lean arms, hugging her tightly while Jillian's sob finally escaped, shaking her body.

"You know, Jillian, it's alright to talk about her. It's healthy, even. I'm glad you're finally starting to open up." Iris' thumbs brushed under Jillian's eyes, smearing away tears too long held back.

"Why don't you take a break? You've really worked very hard here, and you deserve a breather. Why not go and sit out the back for a bit before customers flood in, freaking about last-minute bouquets, teddies, and chocolates." Iris chuckled wryly.

"Happens every bloody Valentine's. The line will be out the door soon, so take a few minutes now. Take a few breaths. And here ..." She pushed the coffee back into Jillian's hands. "You deserve this more than I do."

After adding three heaped sugars to Iris' latte, it was finally sweet enough for Jillian to enjoy. It wasn't her usual, but it was a caffeine injection.

Sinking down in her favourite spot beside the banksias, Jillian slipped *Meet Me in Moonshine* from her bag, the wildflowers pressed gently beneath the cover. Sliding them out, she vowed to press them properly as she eagerly hunted for the little red note once more.

Flicking quickly, she found it exactly where she'd left it – wedged between pages outlining the architectural history and planning of the large gardens that straddled Moonshine's Main Street.

He's a cutie, Jillian thought, finally seeing his note properly. Cut into a wonky heart shape, the red paper asked, 'Be My Valentine?' Turning it over, Jillian expected to see a lengthy note about his highlights of the event out on Wattle Tree Road. He wasted no time.

The best thing about today was you.

Her heart constricted. How would he even know who she was? She still had no clue who he might be, and it was killing her. The next line nearly gave her a heart attack.

I don't even know you, not really, but if you actually came to this crazy event today, for me ... well, I think you must be pretty amazing.
I would love to meet. I think it's time, don't you? 'No time like the present,' they say.

Even though it had been her suggestion, now she wasn't so sure. *Oh, Jesus, what have I done?*

Hands shaking, she somehow managed to calm herself enough to continue reading the note.

Dinner? Friday. Dusk. The Rotunda in Main Street Park.
You bring something to eat and I'll do the same.
Surely, we could survive a meal together?
I'll be the man waiting with bated breath and a rose.
Always,
D- xo

Withholding a squeal, remembering Iris' reaction to her last outburst, Jillian's feet tapped up and down on the floor as she did a little seated happy dance.

"You ready for the onslaught?" Iris called. "I'm about to open up!"

Her boss had been right. Within minutes of the little door sign flipping from 'closed' to 'open', the customers had flooded the store.

Tom, lighthouse keeper of The Moonshine Whine, came in to buy flowers for his wife Delilah. And not half an hour later, Delilah arrived to purchase the exact same bouquet for her 'dear, sweet husband Tom'. If it wasn't so romantic, Jillian might have barfed. The old couple were the epitome of those heart-eyes emojis.

"That's a great love story right there," Iris whispered as Delilah toddled out of the store. "She was meant to marry someone else, you know. Runaway bride. All very hush hush at the time, but they've loosened their lips after fifty years of marriage, so I know snippets."

Iris' gossip was cut short by another customer stepping up to the counter. "You want *more* baby's breath? More than *this*?" She held up a few roses already smothered in the tiny white fluffballs. "Alright, let me look out the back."

As Iris went searching, Jillian called, "Next customer please?"

A tall man in paint-splattered workwear with dust in his hair turned slowly around.

"Daisy?"

"Pig stealer!"

His easy laughter filled her with warmth that had nothing to do with the summer heat. Her eyes flicked over him, messy hair to work-worn boots. *What has he been doing?*

"You ... here for flowers?"

"Uh, yeah ..." His sunburnt cheeks flushed a deeper crimson. The freckles she'd noted yesterday were now chocolate pinpricks hidden in tomato-coloured cheeks. Jillian laughed, pushing a stray tendril of dark hair back from her face.

"I didn't exactly agree to go on a date with you and Porky, you know." *How presumptuous he is!*

"It's, uh ..." Dimples became extremely awkward, eyes on his boots. "It's ... kind of ... not for you ..."

"Oh, Jesus. I'm sorry. I shouldn't have assumed ..." The heat flushed up her body in new and awful ways.

"I kind of have another ... I mean, a *different* date ..."

She had been right. *Birds of a feather* ... This guy was a charmer and shameless flirt, just like Adam James. *You dirty, rotten, greasy, pork-stealing womaniser!* Jillian's mind lashed out aggressively, her carefully placed smile wavering.

"I'm sorry, Daisy, I organised it a while ago and ... well, I didn't expect to meet *you* ..." His hand eclipsed hers, thumb stroking back and forth as his eyes pleaded with her to understand.

"She's someone who was at Moon Shin?" *Why am I even asking?* It didn't matter who he was dating. It was none of Jillian's business.

He paused.

"Yes."

Bloody green-eyed Cat, stealing all my men.

No, not my *men, just ... oh, whatever!* Jillian gave up trying to think.

"It's fine," she said. "I kind of have another date, anyway. I would have felt guilty if I saw you *and him* in one night."

She laughed lightly, despite the twang of pain in her chest. "I'm afraid I'm not good at being a man-eater."

"Hey! Daisy!"

Seriously? Why had Man-Bun shown up, too? Had all of Adam's attractive mates decided to arrive and fluster her at once?

"You're not a man-eater." Dimples said it like it was a fact. The sky is blue. He smelled divine. She wasn't a man-eater.

"Yeah, she'd need a date for that," scoffed an arrogant local lawyer. Jillian recognised him from a series of horrible, cheesy ads he'd taken out in the paper. "Poor love's dry as a desert, anyone can see it. But don't let it stop you from trying. Wet her whistle and the drought will be done!"

Dimples and Man-Bun turned. All legs and breadth and youthful brawn, they stood over the little, blue-suited man, eclipsing him in sheer rage.

"Apologise. *Now*," one of her white knights ground out between clenched teeth.

"Who even thinks it's acceptable to speak to a lady that way?" someone else hissed.

"That's our friend you just insulted, you arse-hat!"

Friend. Her heart sunk further into her stomach.

"S-s-sorry," the jerk mumbled out.

Iris stormed around the counter, scissors in hand. "You leave my store, Dirk West, or I'll lace your current wife's begonias with chilli powder!"

Jillian tripped on air. She'd heard Iris' threats before, but the scene rattled her in a different way.

Dirk? Oh, Jesus, no!

He had a name starting with a D.

Despite the grey sprouting from his temples, the callous lawyer had dark hair. And shrewd, *blue* eyes.

Dirk spun on his smart leather shoes, lips pursed, as every pair of eyes in the long line of customers bore into him.

"For shame!" a woman wearing a baby and a scowl said, swatting the lawyer with her diaper-laden bag. Jillian offered the lady a small smile of thanks.

Blue eyes, dark hair, name starting with D ... This was all getting too much, matching clues to various Moonshine menfolk.

How about Tom and Bre's observation? Her brain tried to calm the rapid beat of her heart. *They both said my Mystery Man was tall.*

Jillian wouldn't exactly describe Dirk as tall, but then, she was wearing wedged heels. If she were flat-footed, he would have been taller than her and really, height judgements were relative, as Bre also noted.

"Another potential ... wasted," she sighed.

"What?"

Man-Bun and Dimples synchronised their attention back to her.

"Never mind. Look, guys, I'm going to let Iris take your orders, okay? See you around."

"Only if you look up." Dimples attempted a joke.

"Wait, Daisy, I–" Man-Bun tried to respond, to reach for her hand and hold her in place, but Jillian was already watching her own feet shuffle from the store.

It had been a long and productive, yet emotionally exhausting day at Bloomin' Brilliant. Nauseating jealousy wore her like a skin suit, after seeing so many people wanting to share their love on Valentine's Day. And after her almost-romantic fail with the dimpled Coffee-Killer, Jillian was feeling deflated but more determined than ever to discover who the mysterious note writer was.

Like a dog with a bone, she wouldn't let it go. An idea had taken root and she was going to fertilise the shit out of it until it came to fruition.

In the air con of her car, where she'd been sitting, thinking, in the hour or so since the florist closed, she slid her phone from her bag.

Breanna, I need that address.

Almost immediately her phone pinged in reply.

> Which one? Sorry, baby brain. I swear the little succubus is stealing my brain cells rather than growing its own.

> The author of Meet Me in Moonshine. I need to know where he lives.

> Need to know? LOL stalker vibes!

> Just call me Nancy Drew. There's a mystery that needs solving and you've got this puzzle piece. I need it. Please? The address?

The three dots indicating Breanna was typing a response bubbled onto the screen, then disappeared. Again, they appeared, then vanished. After an agonising wait, a street address popped up.

> 10 Mundy Street. Go get him, tiger! xo

Jillian clicked on her blinker and started for the address.

The scene in the flower shop had opened her eyes *wide* today. She needed to know who the note writer was. And she needed to know *now*. What would happen, how would she react, if she went to her romantic dinner tomorrow night expecting an Adonis and instead found a Dirk West? She shuddered. *No thank you.*

He didn't even need to be an Adonis. Looks certainly weren't everything. Her Moonshine Mystery Man just needed to *not* be a dick. Before anything else happened (or *could* happen) with this weird relationship they'd weaved of paper and places, she needed to know just a bit more than he was telling her.

Jillian parked a few houses down from 10 Mundy Street, killing the Swift's engine. There it was. The door of the man who'd authored the book clutched between her thighs.

Sliding her hands from the steering wheel, Jillian flicked through *Meet Me in Moonshine*. A collage of black and white images flooded her brain. Why hadn't it occurred to her to check the author's details before?

Turning to the title page, Jillian gasped as a new puzzle piece slid into place.

By Daniel Leas and Declan Smith.

Oh, Jesus! Two D's?

"And – let me guess," she said, sneering at the book's cover, now slammed deftly shut. "They're both tall, dark-haired, blue-eyed lads, who are charming and funny and kind and not at all afraid of spiders, and who go pig wrestling in their spare time ..." Frustrated, she tugged at her dress. The sunflower print was mocking her decidedly *un*-sunny mood.

As she rambled on to herself, a tall, fit man in a baseball cap and sunglasses jogged past her car. He moved so effortlessly, with grace in his movements. She had to stop what she was doing and appreciate it.

Passing through the white picket gate of the property she certainly hadn't been staring at creepily for way too long, he knocked on the heritage-green front door.

"Hey!" she heard a man's voice say, muffled by distance and the car window.

As subtly as possible, she turned the key slightly in the ignition and rolled the window down a crack.

"Ready?"

"Sure thing."

"Let's go."

Their voices were clearer now. *Good*. Turning from the gate, they began to run ... heading straight for her. Like a deer in headlights, she froze, recognising the men almost instantly. The first one, the man she'd ogled as he'd run past, was ... *Oh no, Adam James!* She'd been sucked into his gravitational orbit, just like those silly, jealous girls on the dance floor.

Jillian recognised the other man, too. With intense relief, she realised it *wasn't* Dirk West.

"Man-Bun!" She breathed in awe, watching his long hair, now pulled pack into a ponytail, bounce with each step. The men's heavy footfalls were approaching rapidly as they jogged side by side, matching 'Fit But' shirts hugging their fine forms.

Man-Bun lives at 10 Mundy Street! Holy Jesus! But which author was he? Daniel Leas? Or Declan Smith? Jillian slid down until she was below window level, staying there until she could no longer hear their banter, laughter, or the sound of their steps.

That took longer than expected.

"Hey, wait up!" Man-Bun's voice called.

Oh crap, oh shit, oh fuck!

"Dude, what are you doing?" Adam's laughed query echoed up the street.

Chancing a look, Jillian popped her head up, just a smidge, to peek out the window.

Man-Bun had stopped by a neighbour's house, just outside her car. Gently, he bent over the white picket fence, picking the biggest, most beautiful rose from a bush. Pressing it to his nose, he inhaled deeply, lips curved in bliss.

Are you smelling memories of the Queen's Rose Garden? she wondered, watching his quiet moment of contentment. The last note had said, 'I'll be the man waiting with bated breath and a rose.' Was that The Rose? *Her* rose?

"Coming!" he yelled down the hill to Adam, prompting Jillian to slide back down again. When their footsteps no longer echoed up the street, she braved another peek, finally sitting tall.

"Well then," she said to *Meet Me in Moonshine*, slipping it onto the passenger's seat. "That's interesting."

The Swift revved to life, the 'Bangers' evening radio programme on The Cat and The Fiddle playing to deaf ears.

She'd done it. She'd slotted another puzzle piece into place. And yet, Jillian was strangely disappointed Man-Bun might be *The One*. He was two million times better than Dirk West, but still ... he wasn't Dimples.

The two-timing Coffee-Killer, you mean?!

What was this exercise revealing about her standards in men? Why did she feel deflated by the revelation of Man-Bun at 10 Mundy Street, when her other Mystery Man options had included a rude yet annoyingly perceptive lawyer, an old friend she'd sworn never to sleep with, and a slimy pig stealer. Were these really her only romantic options?

Samuel Harthrup, all floppy blond hair, brown eyes and various stains, slid into her thoughts. *Yeah, okay, okay.* But small-town options weren't all bad ... were they?

Despite all the progress she'd made of late, the familiar loneliness crept in as her gaze swept over her heritage home. She had left the upstairs light on, the chandelier observing the street from its perch in the window. The light trick suggesting someone might be inside this huge, stately house, was a painful lie.

Tonight, she would need a cool, solitary dip in the pool to soothe her. A long soak in the water while she waited, watching her own window at the side of the Maitland Mansion, for the only reliable male in her life to slip into her bed.

Friday

A VALENTINE'S BIRTHDAY

BLOOMIN' BRILLIANT SLAPPED A 'SOLD OUT' sign in the window at 10:04am. At 10:09, Iris flipped the service sign to 'CLOSED'.

"What a hit!" her boss laughed, dancing around the empty storefront. "Best Valentine's Day yet!" She sung the words, shaking Jillian's shoulders.

If only, Boss Lady.

"Got a hot date tonight, Birthday Girl?" Iris asked, handbag already in her hands, eager to leave.

"Not sure."

"Not sure if he's hot, or if it's a date?" Iris' feather-light eyebrow cocked.

"Both?"

"Oh, honey." Iris dropped her keys and handbag. "Tell me everything."

Hours flew as Jillian recounted the entire tale to Iris. The florist sat silent and still, nodding occasionally.
Quietly, she absorbed the story being told in slips of red paper, between the pages of *Meet Me in Moonshine*.

"So tonight, we're supposed to properly meet." Jillian sighed. "And I don't know if the note writer is the author of the book, if Man-Bun is The One, but I cheated in the game, and I don't want him to be equally disappointed in *me* ..."

"Who says he'll be disappointed?"

"Me? Dirk West?" Jillian raised her tear-filled eyes from Iris' sturdy orthotic Birkenstocks.

"Jillian, honey." Iris pulled her close, stroking the length of her dark hair, as her mother used to. "Do not let the likes of Dirk West affect you. You are wonderful. Full of heart and energy and kindness. I know you've struggled to find the light, since your mother's passing, but darling, you have to realise, it's all within you."

Jillian sniffled, sinking further into Iris' embrace. The florist held her tight.

"Sunshine seeps from your very soul, Jillian Maitland. There is absolutely no way this mystery writer, whoever he is, will be disappointed to meet and get to know you." Iris pushed Jillian to arm's length, seeking her gaze. "Look at me, honey. Look at me."

After a long moment, Jillian exhaled slowly, meeting the caramel brown gaze of her employer. "You deserve to be happy, Jillian. You hear me? You deserve all the wonderful things in life."

Jillian sniffed, nodding.

"And I'm going to help you get them."

Never had Jillian worn so much gunk caked on her face. Over the past few hours, Iris had given Jillian a gold-star date treatment. Painted nails, curled hair, carefully applied make-up, and assistance choosing the perfect outfit. Jillian's summer wardrobe consisted almost entirely of floral dresses and sandals, but somehow Iris had found that one little black dress all women apparently had hidden away, pairing it with some pretty accessories that had belonged to Jillian's mother.

"I can't wear these!" she had almost cried on the spot when Iris brought the gems into her room.

"You can and you will. Your mum would want them worn, especially for occasions such as this." Iris slid behind Jillian, gently clipping a pearl drop necklace around her neck. It rested cool and heavy, drawing attention to the cleavage Jillian had tried (unsuccessfully) to shove down into the dress. The girls just kept ... *popping*.

"Happy birthday, sweetheart," Iris whispered, plopping a small kiss high on Jillian's cheek. Just like her mother used to. Affection for this woman swept over Jillian and she swivelled, tackle-hugging her boss, barely holding back the tears threatening to ruin an hour's worth of carefully applied make-up.

"No time for this mushy stuff," Iris laughed, pushing Jillian back. "You need to hurry up. I have a wife at home who I should probably pick some flowers for on my way home."

It was an old joke. Despite owning a florist, Iris always picked fresh flowers from their neighbours' gardens for her wife, Alicia.

"Can't keep her waiting," Jillian said with a smile, inhaling shakily.

Her appearance was good as it was going to get (for an almost-blind date she wasn't sure if she had the stomach to attend). Said gut twisted into knots, wondering if Man-Bun (would he turn out to be Daniel Leas or Declan Smith?) would be relieved or repulsed when she showed up at dusk for their dinner date.

Will I be ... enough? The thought pricked like a thorn in her mind as they clipped into the Swift, starting the engine.

Moments later, a new question kept invading her thoughts.

"How long do we have?" Jillian asked, zipping her Swift in and out of the traffic that had decided to choke Main Street for the first time in, like, *ever*.

"A little over fifteen minutes until dusk," Iris managed between gritted teeth, knuckles white as she gripped the seat sides. "No need to rush, Jillian."

"Every need to rush, Iris," Jillian countered. "Granny May's closed five minutes ago."

Iris hissed as Jillian mounted a roundabout. "Is a pie really this important?"

"Jesus, yes," Jillian spluttered, swinging into a park near Granny May's infamously hidden bakery. Across the road, a thicket of trees hid a corner of the Wollundry River – something she hadn't noticed on her first visit.

Well, my eyes are open now! Pity I don't have time to explore the riverbank.

Jillian would have bet her mother's pearl earrings there was a perfectly shaded picnic spot just beyond those trees. As she shot out of the car, she vaguely recalled an annual school sports day held on Wollundry River.

Despite her love of water, Jillian had never attended. The many stories of bikini-clad classmates told by Adam and Bre painted vivid pictures, though.

If nothing else comes of this adventure, she thought, *if it all crashes and burns tonight, with this date, at least I tried. I did it. I came back to life.* Pride swelled in her already popping chest as she charged towards Granny May's.

"This bakery can't be much chop if I've never heard of it before!" Iris protested, yelling out the wide-open door, watching her employee knock on the store's window, peering in.

"Please!" Jillian called, voice echoing off the glass, "I know you've just shut, and it's Valentine's Day, and you have somewhere to be, and dates to go on because you're very pretty and young …" She was rambling. Rambling like an idiot.

The teenagers inside giggled, opening the door a crack. It was the same girl who had served her earlier in the week. Bethany. For the first time, Jillian took in the girl's pixie-like features, her fine nose, high cheekbones and cropped hair. Faces, she decided, were much more interesting than footwear.

"Please, Bethany," Jillian breathed, her dark curls sticking to the sweat accumulating at the back of her neck. "I just need–"

"We're out of stock," Bethany said apologetically, already closing the door in Jillian's face.

Is this a sign? It must be a sign. I cheated with the scavenger hunt. I worked to identify the mystery writer. I practically stalked him! Then I wasn't very grateful.

I broke the rules. I deserve this.

This is why you don't get your hopes up. Maybe I should just go home, slip into the pool and then snuggle with Oscar, my feline fire-ball.

A hundred different considerations swirled like flimsy petals caught in a tornado.

"Oh, honey, it's fine," Iris said as Jillian slumped back into the driver's seat. "You can take some other food to this dinner. We'll swing by the grocers on the way to Main Street."

"It's not just the pie." Jillian sighed, head wrapped in her arms, leaning on the steering wheel. "It's what it represents." She turned to Iris. "Maybe this is a bad idea."

"Psh!" Iris scoffed. "Bad ideas are for people younger and less intelligent than you. This is a chance. An opportunity. Don't hole up in that shell of yours and let it slip by."

Jillian's eyes moved back to Granny May's Bakery.

"I understand the pie was symbolic," Iris went on. "That's part of the charm of cheap, hand-picked flowers." She smiled, patting Jillian's hair. "But you're on a deadline here, honey. You'd better get going."

Sighing again, Jillian closed the car door and clicked her seatbelt into place.

"You're right, Iris," she conceded. "This *is* a chance. And it was my idea. Whoever this Daniel or Declan guy is, it's not about pie. It's about Spiderman and wildflowers."

Iris' face crinkled in confusion as Jillian prepared to reverse.

"WAIT!" Bethany burst out the door of Granny May's Bakery, a small box in her hand.

Slamming her foot on the brake, Jillian rolled down her window, meeting the girl's eyes.

"It was in the back of the warmer," Bethany said, shoving the small box through the window and into Jillian's hand. "I'm sorry, it's a bit crispy, but the inside will still be good! Free, totally free, even though you're not in the shirt." Bethany took in Jillian's outfit. "Damn! You're looking *hot*! Got a date?"

"I do now." Jillian looked at the gift in her palm. The cartoon image of Granny May herself grinned back at her.

Swapping seats, Iris drove Jillian to Main Street. Trembling, Jillian's hands clutched the box.

The windows of every restaurant and café in town brimmed with couples. Soft lighting, red roses and hearts blessed each low-lit scene.

Moonshine could make an event of a molehill, and this Valentine's Day, Jillian's 30th birthday, was no exception.

Main Street had been decorated with tiny, twinkling fairy lights that peeked through the canopy of leafy trees. Streetlights traced wrought-iron arches above the wide walkways and roads, their dim glow casting a magical spell.

The meeting time – 'dusk' – posed a problem. The sun started sinking in the sky around 5:30pm, finally slipping behind The Whine's barely-a-hill horizon about 7pm. By eight o'clock, dusk will have properly settled, the evening sighing into existence shortly after. That was a wide window, and Jillian hoped she wouldn't be waiting too long. A minute dragged into an hour when anxiety was involved.

And when it was disgustingly hot. Tilting her elbows higher, Jillian forced the cool air to hit her pits.

Iris stopped the car outside Friday's Café, which straddled the huge block of green gardens and grass. The amazing, central location was likely a major factor in the café's success. The other being a quality, sure-fire caffeine hit.

Jillian's eyes wandered away from the park and into her favourite coffee house. While she sat, breathing deeply and gathering her courage, Friday's had sprung to life with its usual 6pm turnover tune. The blaring music reminded Jillian of The Angels backing track that had accompanied the evening she'd met the Coffee-Killer, Dimples.

That feels like a lifetime ago, now.

Friday, unmoving behind his life-giving-caffeine machine, watched, solo, as patrons and staff paired off for a slow waltz to honour the occasion. For a moment Jillian wondered if, perhaps, Friday was her mystery writer.

Is 'Friday' his first or last name? And are his eyes blue? Or ... Jillian pondered, realising she should already know this information about the person she saw the most regularly in this town.

The impact of her social isolation hit like a brick. She knew the exact size, shape, and colour of his Converse All-Star sneakers, but not his actual name or the colour of his eyes. There was something deeply troubling about that.

I should know this stuff, she berated herself. *I need to look up more and connect with people,* really *connect.*

Then, *Could he be my Mystery Man?* Friday would have been perfectly placed to drop *Meet Me in Moonshine* into the MERI book selection. And here he was, alone in a crowd, on Valentine's. He had said he didn't recognise the book, but he may have been fibbing.

But no, that doesn't add up, another part of her brain piped up. It didn't explain the address Breanna had given her. The blue-eyed, brown-haired Man-Bun, with sculpted stubble, curls that kissed his shoulders when he let his hair down, and the intriguing, smile-lined face. The fellow who had left the place at 10 Mundy Street. And, hopefully, she begged the Gods of fashion, the man who *never* wore socks with sandals.

Unless the note-writer wasn't the author of Meet Me in Moonshine *at all?* She sat up straighter.

"Oh, Jesus." Jillian's head started pounding with possibilities, sweat glistening on her skin. Fiddling with the air vents, she fanned herself. "Is it hot? This is, like, the *hottest* summer on record, yeah?" The pie box wiggled as she turned up the fan setting, blasting herself with icy bliss while old Granny May grinned up from her crotch.

Iris laughed. "Sun's going down, honey. It's now or never, so get!"

Jillian dragged herself out of the car.

"I'll drive the Swift to my place, and with any luck your

165

Mystery Man will escort you there *tomorrow* to collect it." Iris winked, driving away before Jillian could counter the plan. "The neighbour's dahlias are calling my name!" she called out the window, speeding off.

Jillian gaped after her car as it disappeared down the long main street.

"Give me strength, mum," Jillian whispered to the purpling sky, one hand on her necklace and the other balancing the small bakery box atop her MERI book treasure. Her wedged sandals clopped lightly as she descended the old stone steps down to the Park.

Moonshine's Main Street Park was lovely during the day, but in the growing evening, it was nothing short of magical.

Glowing, pulsing, fluorescent hearts had been strung high on the wrought-iron lamp poles skirting the park, a loving, glowing fence around the landscaped gardens. As shadows stretched further, the green of the lawns deepened.

The gigantic English oak and liquidambar trees planted by the town's original settlers were hung with tiny lights that glittered like stars, creating subtle shadows, so the trees appeared to be breathing, dancing, *living*.

The pathways had been swept, the garden beds were fresh with colour and care. In the centre of the lush greenery, her destination – the white rotunda – stood proud.

Jillian had been here a million times. She loved hearing the local musicians, who played concerts here year-round. Rain, hail, shine or snow, live music thrummed through the little circular pavilion. Tonight, a soft breeze rustled the trees and happy bugs sang to the encroaching night. It was the most glorious soundtrack imaginable.

Markets and festivals often filled Main Street Park's space and the surrounding streets. She could almost see the bright, cheerful stalls, smell the deep-fried deliciousness coming from the food trucks.

In spite of her shoes, Jillian felt the softness of the grass that had never (to her knowledge) known a weed. The sweet scent of the rose bushes encircling her destination called to her. Guided her home.

Never had she been this nervous in Main Street Park.

The fear of the unknown – no, the *uncertain* – gripped her tightly. Her confidence crashed to the floor. Head down, she moved slowly towards the tall, dark, silhouette of a man leaning against the rotunda railing.

Step. Breathe in. Step. Breathe out.

Somehow, she inched closer until ... *Those shoes.*

"I recognise those shoes," she told them, watching as they rocked back on their heels.

"Hello," said a warm, male voice. She knew he was smiling, because she'd bravely raised her head and was now staring, wide-eyed, into the most gorgeous blue eyes. Eyes she could sink in. Eyes she could swim in, forever.

"It's *you*," she breathed.

"It's you," he echoed, pressing a bouquet of highly scented 'Mister Lincholn' red roses into her free hand. The distinctive ribbon read 'Bloomin' Brilliant'. Her heart leapt against her ribcage. With a laugh, he added, "Thank God it's you!"

Shock rooted her to the spot.

"Of all the almost-thirty-year-old single women in Moonshine ..." His hand brushed her cheek. "I would never have guessed your age, you know. You look younger."

Tingles leapt into her warm cheeks.

Oh, he's a charmer alright.

Jillian mentally ticked 'charming' on her ideal man wish list.

"*Officially* thirty." Jillian leaned closer, almost whispering, "It's my birthday today."

"It is? Seriously? Well! Happy birthday, beautiful."

Closing his eyes, he dropped a tiny, quick kiss on her cheek. Waves of warmth pulsed with each rapid heartbeat; every hair on her body shivered to attention.

"I'm Declan, by the way."

He was close. So close. Real, and *here*. He wasn't some distant note-writing scavenger hunter. Not a spider-battling, wildflower-picking secret lover. A genuine flesh-and-blood man who had boldly expressed loneliness and was working hard to find happiness and connection. Feelings she knew well.

Every clue she'd accumulated in her head crashed together, the dots connecting in her mind. Some pieces of this puzzle still eluded her, but she looked forward to discovering them with this man.

"I'm Jillian."

He raised an eyebrow and she shrugged. His smile tugged wider, meeting his eyes.

"It's lovely to see you again, Jillian," he said, blue eyes searching hers for a long moment before he bent his head, hesitated, then gently pressed his lips to hers.

Every nerve ending in Jillian's skin tingled as heat and longing washed over her. How long since she'd been kissed? Been kissed like *this*? Had kissing always been this good?

"Holy Jesus," she sighed as he stepped back, clearly trying to keep himself in check. "That was ..."

"Yeah." He raked an unsteady hand through his dark hair. "That was ... wow."

"Wait 'til Oscar hears about this," she grinned to herself, hand raised to her lips.

"Oscar?"

"My cat. Well, not *my* cat. He only wants to crawl into my bed at night."

Suddenly, talking about crawling into bed was too intimate, too personal, too flirtatious. Heck, she'd just kissed an almost stranger! And as amazing as that was, she'd built this up so much in her head, she had to be careful.

Don't wreck this before it's even begun! she berated herself, the heavy implication melting away as he grinned at her beneath the twinkling fairy lights.

"Interesting," he said. "I have a cat too, but only during daylight hours. Silver grey. Demanding. Bit of an arsehole, to be honest."

Jillian's mouth dropped to her sandals. *No way! It couldn't be ...*

"Oscar, you rascal!" she smiled, eyes locked with Declan's. Light flecks streaked his dark blue eyes, his pupils seemed to darken as he smiled down at her.

Looking for some way, *any* way to break the tension that sizzled between them, Jillian spluttered, "You look nice."

She stepped back, eyes sweeping over him slowly, taking in every detail.

He had dressed up for their date. Long black dress pants, despite the sticky summer heat, and a button-down shirt with the sleeves rolled up. The shirt hugged the curve of his biceps, and Jillian found her eyes travelling down, savouring the form of him like she hadn't dared on their previous encounters.

Bre was right – he'd look amazing in a swimsuit. His thigh muscles ran long and lean through the dark pants. The buckle of his belt glinted, reflecting the minimal light left in the world.

He caught her staring at his crotch and laughed as he took her hand.

"You look ..." his eyes travelled over her, "just ... wow. Seriously, Jillian, you're a knock-out." His gaze swept down, lingering on her lips, her breasts, her hands.

"What's this?" he asked, stroking her fingers that still held the Granny May's box between them.

"I ... I brought you something." Beneath his warm touch, her hands shook. "You did say to bring dinner." Jillian pushed the bakery box closer.

His smile curled into a grin as he took her offering. Inhaling deeply, he opened the box. His jaw dropped, and the air shifted suddenly.

A shiver ran down her spine.

"What? What is it?" Jillian pulled the pie into view, expecting it to be smashed.

It's fine. Totally intact!

"What's wrong?" Confusion crinkled her brow.

Declan laughed. *Laughed!* Loud and deep and true. It drew her in; she giggled, then shook with laughter, snorting as she tried to get herself under control.

Leaning on each other, they filled the dusk with delight; a pleasant ache settled in Jillian's cheeks. *I love this. I hope we laugh this easily forever ...*

"Do you ..." He hiccupped, wiping at his eyes. Those blue, blue eyes. "Do you know what this is?"

"The last available offering, I'm afraid." Jillian grinned up at him, gripping her roses. "I had to beg for the last pie."

His arm slid around her, pulling her close to whisper into her ear.

"It's ..." he chuckled again. "It's ..."

"Yes?"

"Pork!"

Epilogue

Skinny Dipping

LAUGHTER RANG OUT ACROSS the rippling surface of the water as they cannon-balled, naked, on loop. Holding their knees high and tight, laughter and squealing filled the night.

Thank God I have high fences and deaf old neighbours, thought Jillian, grinning wildly into the night.

"I feel like a teenager again," she said, sweeping her arm wide to scoop a wall of water in his direction.

"Yeah, well, you are officially a nanna now, you know, Miss It's-My-Birthday-Today," Declan teased.

Declan ... her note-writing Mystery Man had a name. More than that, he had dragged Jillian out of her doldrums and back into an engaging and exciting world.

What a difference a few weeks can make ...

In a remarkably short time, she had made the decision to bravely engage with people again, thanks to the gentle encouragement and adventurous nature of this man.

Adventurous is one word, she thought, watching his slippery form glide from the ladder as he hauled himself up, preparing to douse her with another cannonball. She had purposely kept the lights off, affording them added privacy – a decision she regretted immensely.

By the light of the night alone, her eyes strained to seek more. Every dip and curve and solid plane of his body was merely a slip of light. A sliver of an edge, shifting in tiny increments as he rapidly hurled himself into the pool once again.

She couldn't remember whose idea the midnight swim had been. Maybe hers? She did end up here most evenings, washing the day's stress away, thinking too much, and avoiding the stuffy, lonely house.

Not so lonely anymore.

She grinned up at Oscar, who was peeking curiously at them from her second-storey window. Nosy by nature, she bet he saw all from that perch.

The circling light of The Moonshine Whine caught her attention. If one eye saw all, it was the random lighthouse, watching over the Moonshine residents every night without fail. The Whine saw them, exposed to the stars, together. No longer alone.

But whose idea had it been to skinny dip? Surely not hers. She wasn't *that* brave. But if he had been the one to suggest getting naked for a swim, how had he managed to convince her to participate? Jillian hadn't been naked in front of a man in … *Oh, Jesus* … a long time.

She let out a long, low exhale. Goosebumps rippled across her skin and she sunk deeper, her chest dipping below the water.

Let's not think bout that right now, she told herself, grinning as Declan advanced, an evil glint in his shadowed eyes.

"What?" she said, unable to stop her face mirroring his wicked smile.

"Oh, nothing. Just wondering what you're pondering so quietly in the corner."

Right now, all Jillian *wanted* to ponder was how to slow her rapid heartbeat, which pulsed, heavy and warm and shockingly low in her body. And how to stop herself from doing something they might regret.

Despite the intimacies and truths they had expressed in their notes, and over their long Valentine's dinner (though neither had eaten the pork pie, agreeing it would be immensely wrong on so many levels), Declan Smith and Jillian Maitland still barely knew each other. They shouldn't be up to the naked part of their relationship. Yet here they were, barely hiding their wobbly bits as they took turns to bombard the other with midnight waves.

"Just thinking about my cat." *Oh, great. Smooth one, Jillian.*

"I was thinking about that too." Declan splashed her lightly, teasingly, as he swam closer. The outline of him, just a head and overlapping, concentric ripples on an inky black surface, advanced slowly. "You think our arsehole pets are one and the same?"

As if to discourage the humans from discovering his own Moonshine adventures, Oscar meowed loudly down to their dark shadows in the pool.

Jillian erupted into laughter, her cheeks already aching from their new, unfamiliar exercise.

"This is all just too weird," she said, smiling up to the stars. The full moon had faded last week, but the night sky in this town had a magical shine of its own. The Milky Way snaked lazily above, splitting time into 'then' and 'now'.

Two weeks ago, if someone had told her she'd have a naked man in her pool, a man she had feelings for, because of some random notes shoved in a book, spilled beer, a small bunch of wildflowers, and a *greasy pig* (for Heaven's sake!), she would have exploded Vesuvius-style into snorting laughter. While staring at their shoes. Those things did not a romantic story make.

But two weeks was a lifetime. A million little moments ago.

Declan's warm hands found her, sliding through the water to circle her arm and drag her closer, very slowly. Time stood still, now, beneath the stars.

The cool water kissed her tingling skin as she floated gently towards him, the memory of his cheeky birthday kiss still hovering on her lips. His hands, warm in the cool water, held hope.

Realising the last thing his hand had touched was his crotch, she felt heat rise to the surface of her skin. Despite the darkness, he'd clasped his hands modestly in front of himself as he'd jumped into the pool, causing a tidal wave that sent her spluttering into retreat.

In the dark, Declan Smith was a fine-cut silhouette. Lean and strong and sure. She'd only caught a glimpse – just a peep – of his downstairs region as he'd slid off his black dress pants, relishing the fresh air on his legs. Now he was only an occasional line of light reflected off the surface of the pool, but *damn*. Dimples was an attractive man.

It was a typical Australian summer night, all sweat and cicadas, but Jillian shivered like a leaf as Declan pulled her to within an inch of his body, the water warming and electrified between their barely separated skin.

"Do you know how long I've waited to meet you, Jillian? To feel this–" he inhaled deeply, then his exhale sent another wave of tingles down to her core, "–alive?"

"How long?" she breathed into the space between them, watching the starlight play at the sides of his mouth; on the two shadowy dimples she longed to touch.

"Long enough, I think," Declan said, hesitating only slightly before pressing warm, wet lips to hers.

Energy surged through her. Deepening the kiss, ravenous, demanding, she drew herself closer, sharing the warmth of his chest while his circling hands washed cool water at her back. The difference in temperature was dizzying. Declan pushed them to the side of the pool, seating Jillian on the ledge.

Tiny rocks pressed into her bare backside, but she barely registered their imposition. Declan's hands rose from the water, sliding up her neck and holding her jaw softly, while his tongue dived deeper for more. Her knees clenched at his waist and Jillian broke the kiss, needing to breathe.

"Shit, sorry," he said. Cold water washed her as he retreated. "Daisy, I'm such an idiot. I'm rushing this, I'm sorry. I–"

"Jillian," she corrected quietly, her breathing shallow.

"What?"

"It's Jillian, Coffee-Killer. Not Daisy. She was the old me. This ..." She looked down at herself, slick and slender, bathed in starlight. "This is someone entirely different."

"Someone with equally short shorts, though, I hope?"

Declan laughed, his dimples catching the light.

"Gotta give the people what they want," Jillian said, smirking. She propelled herself away from the ledge. Her bare skin met his once more, a slow-motion slap beneath the water's surface. Slippery and satisfying, she half drowned, half kissed him.

Moaning, Declan pressed her right back, the heat in his flesh hardening into something else entirely. He manoeuvred his hips away, attempting to hide his erection.

Jillian registered his movement, aware this could get ... *awkward*. Too awkward, too quickly. But her head and her body weren't communicating right now, and her hands slid down to gently cup his backside.

He moaned into her mouth, lapping at her tongue, and she relished the taste of him. Hunger bit at them both as they nipped and sucked, licked and savoured the other's kisses, learning each other's secrets. Water sloshed between them, little lapping sounds filling the night as arms rose and fell, fingers slipped and gripped, kisses met and urged and soft laughs were shared.

"Are you real?" he whispered into her hair, nuzzling his way down her neck.

"Dear Jesus, I hope so." Jillian pressed herself closer, his erection now making itself well known against her hipbone. He throbbed against her skin, hard and hot and present. Her legs laced through his, hips settling at his thighs.

"I think this is a bad idea," Declan breathed against the column of her neck, his trembling hands circling her shoulders, pressing her chest closer to his warm mouth. "I don't want to fuck this up."

"I completely agree," Jillian sighed. A hazy voice in her head was chanting, *Ain't no one who can stop this now.*

Declan had extremely kissable lips. Soft and slick and perfectly moulded to hers. Their puzzle pieces just ... clicked.

Gripping the sides of his head, she pushed back, admiring him. Those dimples caught her eye again and she allowed herself a moment to trace them slowly with her fingertips, as she'd dreamed of doing since they'd met. His grin deepened those valleys.

Despite the literal cheek of the man, his sincere eyes caught hers.

"Want me to back off?" he asked, between ragged, shallow breaths, his body still solid and wrapped in hers. "I will. No questions asked, Jillian."

"I believe you," she said, hands sliding down his chest. She liked the feel of the little hairs she found there, swaying and soft in the water's motion. She wondered how dark they were, vowing to find out, come sunlight. "You have a good heart, Declan Smith."

Her hands travelled lower, slowly. His breath caught. "But right now –" she teased the patch of hairs below his belly button, "I just really want you to be *here*, you know? Alive. Present. With me." Jillian curled her palm around the length of him. Declan jolted at her touch. His eyes still locked with hers, he pushed her against the pool's edge, hips pressing hard to seize her hand between them.

"Jillian, I–"

She silenced him with a kiss, hoping, begging, *praying* he wouldn't back out now. If he did, she might die of mortification. Of unattractiveness, of–

"I want this," she whispered. "Please, Declan."

"Oh, thank God." He sighed. In one swift move, Declan slid his hands under Jillian's thighs, hoisting her up and settling himself between her legs. The tiny rocks scratched at her shoulder blades. The pool shivered with the motion.

Their eyes met and she nodded, her forehead against his as he gently lowered her down, filling her with warmth as their bodies connected.

"Holy shit," she breathed, catching his lip in her teeth. He held still – as still as he could – while a heavy, thick pulse echoed out from between her legs.

"How?" he wondered, breathing hard as he searched her gaze. "How have you been here in Moonshine, right under my nose, all this time?" He thrust himself deeper and she gasped.

Jillian rocked her hips back, and he sighed deeply, his eyes closing as she brought herself forward once more. One, two ... she repeated the slippery motion, his hands biting into her skin.

"Fuck, Jillian ..." his forehead met hers, their breath mingling as she moved. "You're more than I'd let myself hope for, you know that?" He pushed deeper, slow and deliberate, as he caught her mouth in his. Within her, she felt the conviction of his words.

This is perfect. So ridiculously, maddeningly perfect. But ...

The pace was slow, but it was all happening too fast.

Trembling, she slowly rose off Declan, cold water swelling around her again.

"I'm here. I've always been here," she said, laughing into the evening as she rose from the pool with a wicked grin. "Come find me, Dimples."

She giggled down at him. "Meet me in Moonshine."

Jillian took a few slow steps until her feet met dry ground, then ran naked towards the house.

"Come find me!"

"Challenge accepted, Daisy!" he called, racing to catch up.

They disappeared into the old Maitland Mansion where their cat, Oscar Wild, purred merrily from the bed.

The Moonshine series of romances are
standalone, interconnected stories.

Want to know what happens with Jillian and Declan
after Valentine's Day ends? Want a hint into the next book?

Read on...

A Year Later

"DID YOU HEAR THEY had a *pig* at the wedding?" Mrs Henderson hissed to Mrs Miller, shuffling forward a half-step in the line.

"I heard it was the flower girl ... er, flower *pig*," Mrs Miller whispered back. "Strapped a basket of petals to its back and set it loose in the church!"

"Good heavens, surely they didn't!"

"They *did*! That Billy Carmichael confirmed it. He was there, bless his soul. A 'whirlwind romance' they said, though there are whispers of a baby on the way. I mean, it has only been a few months, really! But they're *madly* in love. It's obscene."

"Obscene," Mrs Henderson echoed.

"Though I'm glad Mister Carmichael attended the wedding. Nice to hear he stepped under the Lord's roof again, since his *accident*."

"Oh, dear, I do recall it! In the paper for *weeks*, it was."

"And running that bar," Mrs Miller *tsk*ed. "We thought he'd fallen off the wagon *entirely*, didn't we?"

"Oh, and didn't she look lovely!"

"Who?"

"The *bride*, dear. Jillian Maitland. Well, I suppose it isn't *Maitland* anymore, is it?"

"I remember the day of their wedding," Mrs Henderson sighed. "I saw the groom before the ceremony. Grinning like a monkey, he was. Those dimples! Oh, what a strapping young man! Reminds me of my Edgar."

"What does he *do* exactly? Mr Smith, that is. Not Edgar." Mrs Miller slid another step towards Friday. The busy barista smiled up at them briefly.

"Fresh damper with cream and jam today, ladies! Just how you like it."

"You're a *Saint*, Mr Friday!" Mrs Millar crooned, batting her eyelids, before resuming the hushed conversation with her friend. She may as well have been whispering into a megaphone. "Well, I heard he's some kind of *historical architect* or *restoration specialist*," she said, making air quotes with her fingers. "A fine thing, too. Jillian needed help with that huge old house. Wayne Wilson isn't as young as he used to be, you know."

"Wayne's her stepfather, right? Oh, and did you hear they're converting it into a hotel?"

"I did! Declan Smith, *does* that, you know. He and his business partner wrote a *whole book* about the projects they'd worked on in town."

"Oh, yes. They work from an office suite up in Mundy Street, yes?"

"That's *right*, dear. Bought it a while back, I believe. Work for the Council they are, maintaining Moonshine's buildings and working with the Heritage mob ..."

The two old ladies continued their verbal tennis match as they worked their way closer to the counter at Friday's Café. Now that life was returning to normal in Moonshine, after the government imposed COVID lockdown, everyone seemed to be out and about. People were everywhere, catching up on the *who* and *what* and *when* of their missed face-to-face gossip time.

The township was waking from slumber, patrons rushing to Main Street, clogging the streets and stores.

Mrs Miller and Mrs Henderson chatted on about everyone else's business.

They didn't see Samuel Harthrup curled in the corner, scribbling into a tattered notebook. Pencil to paper, he was so absorbed in his work he didn't even hear his phone ringing. Persistently.

"SAM!" Friday barked from behind the counter, catching everyone off guard with his unusually aggravated tone. Friday was always the epitome of cheerful customer service. "Answer your phone or I swear to WHOEVER your God is, it's going to die a painful, SLOW death in my new cold-drip coffee maker!"

All eyes turned from Friday to Sam.

"Shit, sorry Friday. Sorry everyone." Fumbling for the phone, Sam saw '5 missed calls' splashed across the cracked, smudged screen.

It started ringing again, the words 'Doctor Dickhead' flashing persistently. With a sigh, Sam answered.

"Hello, loser."

"Dude, where the heck are you? I came by your flat and you're OUT? Good for you! Where are you? Are you okay? Need some company?"

The excited voice of Reece Hargraves, the biggest pain in the ass and his Best Friend Forever, nearly deafened him. Reece was not a loser, not by a long shot. He'd excelled at every damn thing he'd ever put his hand to, making 'loser' the perfect nickname.

"I'm fine," Sam snapped. "And even though you didn't ask, I'm *sober* and I'm ..." he dropped his voice to a whisper, glancing around him, "I'm writing."

"Writing? Good on you, man! Seriously, well done. It is my professional opinion, as your doctor and best friend for life, that you can kick this book's ass. You're a *great* writer, even though lady porn isn't really my style of literature ..."

"SSSHHHHH!!!" Sam whispered aggressively into the phone, causing the people at the next table to turn.

"Dude, I'm not on loudspeaker, am I? There's no way you need to shoosh me. Nobody's going to hear you're working on the next heart-throbbing plot-to-end-all-plots. Women love that shit. Me? I prefer video format."

Then, before Sam could get a word in edgeways, Reece added, "Don't describe cock as an eggplant. That shit's scary if you think about it. Like, seriously, from a medical standpoint ..."

While Reece blabbed on, Sam tried hard *not* to imagine a life-sized aubergine penis, inflated and purple. His dick winced in sorrow. Sighing, he pinched the bridge of his nose, his spectacles riding high on his brow line.

The door opened and more customers swarmed in.

The air changed. Something smelled ... off.

"Meet me later for a few beers?" Reece continued. "Totally closely monitored and moderated by your favourite doctor, of course. Got a new home brew ready for testing."

"Sure," Sam mumbled, sniffing his shirt suspiciously. *Yep, it's me. I'm The Smell.* Mentally, he added 'washing' to his to-do list. *Shit.*

"Sweet. I'll leave you to your writing, Sammie. Love you."

"Love you, loser," Sam ground out, ending the call whilst pondering on when he'd last done laundry.

Better buy some stain remover.

Sam sighed. If this is what it was like being sober, being productive, being out in the fresh air rather than his dingy, grey-walled cave of an apartment, he wasn't sure if he liked it.

This was surprisingly difficult. It was too ... *bright*, out here in the real world. Too much reminded him of *her*.

Although it was a small town, Moonshine was just too big for the space in the universe he wanted to occupy right now.

Pushing his fingers under the thick rims of his spectacles, Sam dug his fingers into his eye sockets, breathing deeply.

I need to get my head straight. I need to write this book, and I need to pay my mountain of bills, and I can't do it like last time. I can't get wrapped up in a woman's legs and find inspiration there. Or in the bottom of a bottle.

This time, I'll do the write thing the right way.

There was only one thing for it. He needed to knuckle down, ignore the world, and just write. Sex, love, food, sexy food love. All of it needed to get out of his head and into the novel he'd promised his editor.

No more daytime TV cooking shows and hazy-lensed dramas. No more bad food. He was going to be an adult. Look after himself. Get his business affairs and life in order.

Finally... Hopefully.

I can do this.

Sam stepped out of Friday's and walked up Main Street. It was a new day and he was turning a new page. No temptation, just typing. A new man, a new manuscript.

Nothing was going to stop him.

Nothing would get in his way.

"I can do this!"

"Ooh, look, Mummy! The circus is coming to town!" A gangly child in dirty overalls pointed to a flyer. Drawn by the colourful images, Sam joined the throng of people peering at the large poster, pinned neatly to the community billboard.

She's pretty, a voice in his head commented, as his eyes were drawn to the shapely figure deliciously dominating the centre of the page. Dark-haired and dazzling in her sequined outfit, the woman danced the tango in a striking blue spotlight.

Her partner, a serious, top-hatted ringmaster with equally dark features, stared coolly from the page, the perfect ice to temper her heat. Clowns, acrobats and a huge, roaring lion also featured in the advertisement.

I wonder if they really have a lion. Few modern circuses had wild animals these days, particularly exotic cats.

Sam's eyes swung back to the woman. She was, both literally and metaphorically, *dazzling*.

His zipper suddenly needed adjusting. The notebook felt slick in his cold, sweaty palm.

Tearing his eyes from the image, and working desperately to erase her smooth, tempting curves from his memory, he made a beeline for his shit-box of a car, mumbling.

"Okay, Sammie. Here we go again ..."

Read more of Sam's story in

The Write Way For Love by Brooklyn Dean.

Acknowledgments

Acknowledgements are hard, guys. There are so many people whose energy and love goes into making a book baby. But I'll (try to) keep this short and sweet.

Thank you to my parents:
Mum, thank you for encouraging my passions and simply being there, always, for your eternal support and for being my first reader. Dad, thank you for the storytelling that has been a constant inspiration to me, for being unashamedly you, and for introducing me to greasy pig chases. I am blessed to be your bub.

Thank you to my annoyingly supportive husband:
You bought the laptop that facilitated this dream, you big enabler! Therefore, it's all your fault. Thank you for allowing me to live in my head and at my computer, and for your constant encouragement.

Thank you to my cheerleaders:
Cassie, Melissa, Rachel, Beth, Louise and Annemarie. Your guidance, thoughts, random 2am emoji reactions, gushing and guidance keep me going. You give me strength and direction. Thank you.

Thanks also to my editor:

Sue Copsey. You paired back the melodrama of my characters and made editing something to giggle about. Thank you for helping to settle the words into their final form.

And lastly (but not certainly least) thanks to YOU, dear reader, to whom I am eternally grateful. If you're reading this, then you took a chance on me and my writing (and heck, you even made it to the end)! I hope I didn't disappoint.

I look forward to meeting you back in Moonshine soon!

Liked this book?

Please share your thoughts and leave a kind review!

Whether on Amazon, Goodreads, an email to the author,
a recommendation to a friend, or all of the above.

Like water to a flower, reviews help authors grow!

Thank you.

About The Author

BROOKLYN DEAN is a perpetual daydreamer from rural Australia. She lives with her super supportive husband and children, and a sock stealing Labradoodle named Noodle.

When she's not writing, Brooklyn is often training to become the world hugging champion, drinking coffee, throwing her head back in laughter, or stealing time to nap in the sun.

Connect with Brooklyn on social media:

Welcome to Moonshine

Other books in the Moonshine Series:

- Meet Me in Moonshine

- The Write Way for Love

- The Insufferable Adam James

- A Merry Little Christmas Contingency

Writing about intimacy can be awkward, but someone's gotta do it ...

Samuel Harthrup — AKA romance novelist Sammie Hart — has lost his mojo. His sexy MasterChef-inspired smash-hit *Heat in the Kitchen* left readers voracious for a sequel, but Sam's muse ran off with a hulking, tattooed biker, and his new manuscript is more fizzle than sizzle. Sam needs help – a special ingredient to inspire the spicy scenes his editor (and career) demands. When the circus rolls into the small town of Moonshine, Sam stumbles upon Anita Fortuna, a psychic who firmly believes that wishing upon a star will make your dreams come true. Together, they resolve to whip his manuscript into shape, and succumbing to personal temptations is not an option – no matter how enticing the offer might be.

On a deadline, and with Sam's career at stake, can Sam and Anita find the write way for romance, define their own stories, and discover whether words are enough? Or is the whole deal a recipe for disaster?

The Write Way for Love is a dual POV Aussie rom com with an adorable beta hero and a curvy FMC. If you like cheesy food puns and found family, this interconnected standalone will be to your taste.

ISBN: 978-0-6456910-2-3 (PRINT)

ISBN: 978-0-6456910-3-0 (EBOOK)

One immature dare.
Two childhood enemies.
Three kisses to bring him to
his knees ...

Clarissa Wilson hates Adam James – his dentist-white smile, his ridiculous body built of muscles-upon-muscles, and that movie-star swagger that carries him into every room. So, back in their hometown of Moonshine – sixteen years later – with a revenge body and a new name, it's a guilty thrill when Adam wants her ... and has no idea she's the chubby girl he teased throughout school. As 'Lissy,' she's determined to live life by her own rules and hide her old scars – meaning she needs a plan to deal with Adam, their past, and the present. Luckily, his cheeky dare offers Lissy the perfect opportunity for payback: she has three kisses, and three chances to seduce the man who ruined her life ... then leave him in the dust. But Adam is playing with her heartstrings and rewriting their history, revealing things aren't what they seem. Now, Lissy must decide who she really is and what her heart desires, because three kisses can't undo a lifetime of hate ,,, right?

The Insufferable Adam James **is a dual POV enemies-to-lovers rom com with a droolworthy MMC and a sassy FMC who isn't afraid to speak her mind. If you like banter and secret cinnamon rolls, this interconnected standalone is for you.**

ISBN: 978-0-6456910-4-7 (PRINT)
ISBN: 978-0-6456910-5-4 (EBOOK)

All they want for Christmas is ...

Breanna Henderson lives by lists, strict schedules, and preparations galore. Being pregnant while climbing up a ladder into her best friend Billy's bedroom was definitely NOT part of the plan. This Christmas, everything has changed, and Breanna's meticulous agenda has disappeared out the tinsel-trimmed window.

Billy Carmichael loves the festive season: his family descending on the Christmas tree farm, long days among the pines, and long nights between the sheets with his best-friend-with-benefits, Breanna. But Billy soon discovers that this year, unwrapping his favourite present won't be so easy.

A flirty TV car show host, a celebrity home stylist, and a meddling clan of kilt-loving lumberjacks threaten everything they knew. And then there's the truth about Bre's baby daddy. Billy and Breanna don't just need a Plan B. They need

... A Merry Little Christmas Contingency

A Merry Little Christmas Contingency is a dual POV friends-to-lovers rom com that begins in the bedroom and is full of found family. With a summer Christmas – featuring ZERO snow – anxiety rep and limb difference, this festive story is an interconnected standalone that will fill your heart with Christmas spirit, no matter what time of year it is.

ISBN: 978-0-6456910-6-1 (PRINT)
ISBN: 978-0-6456910-7-8 (EBOOK)

WTP

Wattle Tree Press is an independent publisher located on the picturesque Central Coast of Australia. WTP believes that everyone has a story (or two) within them and aims to bring Aussie storytelling to the wider world.

Their growing catalogue can be found at:

www.wattletreepress.com